THE WHITFIELD RANCHER BOOK 4

KATHI S. BARTON

This is a work of fiction. Names, characters, places, and incidents are products of the author's imagination or are used fictitiously and are not to be construed as real. Any resemblance to actual events, locations, organizations, or persons, living or dead, is entirely coincidental.

World Castle Publishing, LLC
Pensacola, Florida
Copyright © Kathi S. Barton 2018
Paperback ISBN: 9781629899947
eBook ISBN: 9781629899954
First Edition World Castle Publishing, LLC, September 17, 2018
http://www.worldcastlepublishing.com
Licensing Notes
Cover: Karen Fuller
Editor: Maxine Bringenberg

Chapter 1

The house was coming along nicely but Adam still had a few things to get. He'd not thought of the size of the living room when he'd ordered the couch or loveseat, nor the two large armchairs. It could use more furniture.

Hitting the light switches at the panel, he watched as each of them went on and off with the different buttons. Whoever had built this house, had added a lot of little extras like that. Adam didn't remember his grandparents ever mentioning it, but since they'd lived here a long time before he was born, it had never occurred to them to tell him that the switches controlled the lights — not magic as he'd thought when he was younger.

Going out to enjoy the nice warm morning, he sat on his back deck and relaxed in the double sized rocker, giving it a little motion. Josh and Carter were due home in a few days, and he couldn't wait. The two of them had been sending pictures of what they had seen, and he was glad for them both.

Adam had invited his family over tonight, and they thought they were going to enjoy some takeout at his home. He was as excited about that as he'd been in a long time. But little did any of them know, he was ready for a large meal. None of them knew that he'd bought new things and hired a staff.

The cook, Nate Turtle, was an old buddy of his grandda's. He'd told him what he was up to, and the man thought it was a hoot. Adam supposed that he'd have to get used to having the man around. He thought the man talked as much as his grandda did, and he sounded just like him too.

Going into the house, Nate asked him if he wanted anything to eat. "I don't think so. Not now, anyway. I'll just eat a big lunch since I need to go over the books for the ranch, as well as see to it that the rentals I have are up to par."

"You should eat, Adam. If Ollie were to find out you were skipping meals, he'd have both our hides. Now come on and sit down while I make you a manly breakfast." Adam didn't have any idea what that might entail, but he was up for it. "Just tell me how you want your eggs cooked."

Adam had lost some weight because in the summer months all the way to fall he was busy all the time. Pulling out his phone, he ordered two more chairs and looked over bedroom sets, comforter and all, to find one that he liked. His mom would murder him if he bought this stuff half willy, as Grandda said all the time.

The breakfast was huge. Adam stared at it for a long time before he glanced at Nate. He asked him who he was feeding with this much food and Nate only tsked at him. Adam had been relieved when Evan showed up and took half the meal, but it was still too much for both of them.

"I need a favor from you. It's not so much a favor as it is a question for you." Adam asked Evan what he needed from him. "I'd like to go in with you as an equal partner on setting up a hotel."

"I'm buying a hotel?" Evan nodded as he ate one of the

four eggs on his plate. "I don't know if you've noticed this or not, but I'm a farmer, not someone that can run a hotel. I don't have time to work out the plans for one. I just got things here organized enough for me to have a real bed in my room."

"You only have to go in on half. I have the money, but I think it would be more fun if you and I had a project together." He eyed his brother and asked what was really going on. "All right. I'm bored out of my mind—not at work, but at home. Dylan is working on this thing that takes her to some places I can't go, and she might have to do something with someone to take them down. The boys are in school all day. Grandda has that job working in the diner, and Mom has those fundraisers she always does."

"Evan, what makes you think that owning and operating a hotel is going to help you with your boredom? I mean, that sounds like a lot of work. I've been by the one that used to be in town. It's closed down and has been for about a decade. It'll need a total upgrade." Adam felt excited about it but wanted to make sure that Evan was really serious about this and not just shooting bullets—another thing that Grandda said. "I'm great with going in on this with you, but you know that we won't be able to do anything, like renting rooms, until summer, right?"

"I know. But seriously, I need this. And I think you do as well. This is downtime for you, and I think you might like it so much that you won't want to plant come spring." He told Evan that wasn't possible. "We'll see. By the way, there is another doctor that just arrived the day before yesterday—a Doctor Walton. She saved Mr. Williams's life. He had a heart attack, and she was there with him to give him CPR right away."

"What's she in town for?" He told him what her sister had told Dylan. "So, she's just breezing through? That sort of sounds lame. Where is she headed to if she's not staying?"

"Why the third degree? Is it because you're thinking one of them might be your mate? Now that would work out for me a great deal." Adam told him he was glad that he could accommodate him. "You know what I mean. Since I took over as head of surgery, I've not had a lot of time to do operations. It would be nice to have a good doctor that can take up some of my slack for a change."

Adam knew that his brother was overworked, which confused him as to why he'd want to do this hotel thing. When he was on his way out of the house, Evan turned back to him with a smile on his face. Adam had already figured out that he'd bought the hotel and had a crew working on it.

Evan was pouting when he drove off, and Adam was glad to have been able to burst his brother's bubble with his last bit of information. Going to the garage, he was startled when he came upon someone lying in the hay that he'd laid out for the cows for later today.

"May I help you? You do know that you're trespassing, don't you?" She nodded but didn't say anything. "I don't mean to be rude, but what the hell are you doing in my barn at seven in the morning?"

"I'm looking for Tanner." He didn't say that he knew him. Adam wasn't sure that he should anyway. "He's my maker — or I thought he was for a very long time. Like recently. I was wondering if he was about. I have been searching for him for a very long time."

He reached out to the old vampire and told him what he had in his barn, as well as what she'd told him about Tanner being her maker. When he laughed, Adam let out a long breath. He was glad to have something go right. And it was only seven, as he'd told her before.

Is her name — ? Let me think a moment. Ah yes, Wanda. Ask her

8

please. And in the meantime, I'm sending Flora to you. She knows her as well if it is indeed Wanda. Adam asked her what her name was, confirming it was Wanda just before Flora showed up. Tanner spoke again. *She is mistaken about me making her, however. I was only there when she woke, and she has blamed me since. I have no idea what reason she has for coming here.*

I'll find out and let you know. Right now, her and Flora are catching up. But it seems as if Flora is inclined to tell her that you're here. He told Tanner what she'd said about mistaking him for her maker.

I'm coming since the sun isn't too bright yet that I can't come to you.

Tanner was standing next to him just as he finished talking. Adam had asked him once how he could travel so quickly. Adam had to ask and had learned that Tanner didn't just disappear and reappear as everyone thought.

"I can travel at a very high rate of speed—much too fast for a human or anyone younger than me to see. If you were to picture me while I'm moving, you'd see a slight blur and nothing more." He told him that electronics were vastly improved nowadays. "Yes, I suppose that they have. But why would anyone be looking for a vampire? I mean, we're not real to a great many people. Wanda, it's been a very long time. How are you faring?" She stood up and looked at Adam, then at Tanner. "He belongs to me, as does his entire family. You touch one of them without permission, then I will kill you."

"I've no wish to touch the big tiger. But I'm in trouble and I know not how to fix it." She turned then, and he saw the blood that was streaming down her back from a wound up by her hairline. "My master, he called to me. When I refused to do as he wished, I was punished. I only just managed to escape so I could warn you, my lord."

9

"Is Randal still looking for me? You know that I'm not worried about him, do you not?" She nodded, then shook her head. "Come with me and I'll find you a safe haven. Once you are healed, then we'll talk." She thanked him. "Think nothing of it. If you are in trouble, as you said, then you'll be better at winding your tale around to make me understand."

They disappeared, except for Flora. She came to sit on the corral post that Adam had been working on until dark last night. When she seemed content with just watching him, Adam started to whistle. While he didn't like lots of noise, he did like to whistle old tunes.

"Randal is a vampire." Adam stopped working to look at her. "He is bad news—for humans and paranormals as well. It would have done us all a favor should my master have killed him long ago."

"What's he done? For that matter, why would he hurt one of his children? I thought that was a big rule." She told him it was. "Okay. Perhaps this would go better if I stop asking questions and allow you to speak." He winked at her and she smiled. He could see that she was very nervous about something.

"Long ago, before even trains and cars were around, Randal was friends with my master. Tanner was a good man even then, though he'd not think so. I was being injured by Randal. Many of my kind had been caught and put into a large cage, one that was made especially for fae." Adam nodded, figuring he could ask her what that meant later. "He had torn their wings off, you see, so that the magic could come to him. It would take millions of us to fulfill his need, as I'm sure he knew. Tanner came to see him, and he saw what he was about to do to me. Tearing off a fae's wings is the same as it would be to humans to have all their limbs cut from them."

"How many of you had he injured before Tanner arrived?"

She told him, and he shivered. His sorrow for what had happened was great. "Six hundred of you? I'm so sorry for your loss, Flora. I'm assuming that Tanner somehow had the man stopped by force or asking?"

"He took his kiss. You understand that is what a group of vampires is called, correct?" Adam nodded and asked her how that had happened. "It is easy when you are as old as Tanner. But he quit him as well. Told Randal that should he darken Tanner's place on this earth just once, he would never do it again."

"So the two of you became friends after that. But I'm thinking that there is more to this. Not that taking wings from anyone is all right, but Tanner is a forgiving man. At least he is to us." Flora nodded and moved to the other stall when he did. "I'm only making myself busy work. So, if you'd like to go indoors, I'm sure that we can find you something to eat."

"Nay, this is fine, my lord." Adam asked her what else had happened. "Several years later — I think at least a few decades. I cannot pinpoint that part. Time is my worst enemy when I need to remember something. Anyway, several days after Tanner found his mate, they were out celebrating with myself and the two of them. The restaurant was filled to capacity. A large ship was headed out to sea, and they were enjoying the people who were going to board it."

"This ship, did it go down?" She nodded. "Then it has been a few decades. Okay, go on. I'd like to know what happened to Tanner."

"Tanner was just going about his business. I stayed at the table with Fredrick. The two of us were watching the crowd, caught up in the way they were happy." She looked at the newly filled bins. He'd have nothing to put into them until the spring, and he thought that she knew that he was just wasting time.

11

"The first person that we saw fall was a younger man that was making drinks. I thought him only to have slipped. It wasn't until Fredrick spoke that I realized he was dead. By that time, there were over fifty people on the floor, bleeding out. Randal was walking through the crowd, slicing whomever walked in his path as he made his way to our table. He was there to kill Tanner, because he thought him to have gotten him in trouble with the council. He had, of course. Then the trouble started, worse than before."

~*~

Ivy made her way to the end of the public streets and started back the way that she had come. Jogging was the only thing that she could find that would make her sleep after a surgery, even if it had been an easy one. She looked at the bench that sat in front of the little store and watched as they all waved at her. Not stopping, needing this more than she could say, Ivy waved back but kept going.

Evan had pulled some strings for her. Ivy wasn't sure what that might have entailed, but she was now licensed to practice in Ohio. The last time she'd moved and had to apply for the same thing, Ivy knew that she'd never move again just for that reason. It was a long process, and not working would drive her nuts.

Her home was gone. It broke her heart when she thought of all the little things that she'd collected over the years—her diplomas, for one. There were trinkets that she'd picked up while she traveled after getting out of college. All destroyed because of just one man. Ivy had a doctorate in medicine—surgery actually. She had a masters in languages, and another in children's services.

That last one she'd never used again after the first month. The thought of making sure that children were in a safe place was about as easy as it was for her to stand up to piss—messy and difficult.

Her cell was going off when Ivy turned right and took the bike path for the last leg of her journey. "Walton." She answered every call she got, at home or on her cell, the same way. When the person at the other end asked her to hold, she nearly hung up on them. "Can I help you? If not, don't bother leaving a message. I won't answer it anyway."

This number was private, the only people that had it was her former employer where she'd worked for the last ten years, as well as her new one here. Ivy was leaning toward staying around when a woman finally answered.

"I'm calling from Middleton General. We'd like to ask you if you'd mind cutting your vacation short. You'd be able to take it later in the year, but we're very short-staffed right now." Ivy could almost see Lily putting her name on the schedule before calling her. That was confirmed when she came back on the line. "I have you working on Monday, as well as working in the emergency room for the rest of the week. Wednesday, I have you marked for a double. You will be paid overtime for helping me out with this."

"No. I'm on vacation for a reason, and I have no intentions of cutting it short. I gave you several months to find someone else while I was gone, and you waited too long to cover your own hospital. I'm not going to work that schedule or any other one until I return in November, as I told you when I submitted it and got approval for my time off." Ivy couldn't stand Lily. She was manipulative as well as a bitch. "If that is all you called me for, then I'm hanging up now."

"But as I told you, we're short-staffed." Ivy told her that wasn't her problem. "What am I supposed to tell the sick and downtrodden when can't get them in to see a doctor? Do I tell them it was because you were too selfish to come into work? Where are you, anyway?"

"Nun-ya." She asked where that is. "Nun-ya business. That's where I am. Don't call me again, Lily, or so help me, I'll put in my resignation. Have a good day."

Ivy disconnected the call and let it ring to voicemail while she finished up her run. Doing this every day was what kept her in shape, she supposed, and the extra she did to blow off steam didn't tire or hurt her because of it. Cooling down after finishing up the loop through the woods that Evan had told her about, she walked until she was standing in front of the bed and breakfast that she and her sister had been staying in.

Ivy didn't want to go inside. She'd been cooped up all day yesterday in the hospital, and she needed to have the sun on her face. Of course, they were calling for snow over the next few days—that was the only way that she'd stay inside. The snow and driving in it gave her the willies.

Meghan was just coming out when Ivy was moving up the stone walkway. "I'm so glad to see you finally. You have to go with me to breakfast." She told her that it was only about seven in the morning. "I'm well aware of the time, Ivy, but I've been busy. I have been up all night talking on the phone for you."

"I'm not going to go eat anything with you until I get a shower. And what the hell were you talking about that kept you from your sleep?" Meghan told her that she'd been trying to find out about her insurance on her home. "I've already taken care of that. Yesterday, as a matter of fact while you slept late like I thought you would today."

"Well, you could have told me that." She said that she'd not asked. "Ivy, I swear sometimes that you just like pissing me off."

"I do. I'm going to shower. I can meet you after my shower

or you can wait on me. I don't care which." Meghan huffed at her. "I was thinking that we could eat at the dive we passed out on route seventy. Your choice. But I'm going up."

Peeling off her clothing as she went, Ivy turned on the shower. The water pressure wasn't all that much, but there was plenty of hot water. While she was waiting on it to heat up, she pulled out her cell and looked at the twenty missed calls. And more than likely that many messages as well. Blocking that number, and any others that she could think of coming from the hospital, Ivy looked at the one number that she didn't recognize. The message said it was from Doctor Whitfield.

Calling Evan back after deleting the rest of them, she brushed her teeth. Dylan caught her mid-spit.

"I hope that you're not sick. I'd surely hate to go and get that cleaned up. Puking or even the sound of it can have me gagging in no time." She told her that she was brushing her teeth. "Oh, you're an early riser. Good. I'd like to meet you for a little talk. It can be here at my house or the diner in town. I'm good with either."

"Town. My sister feels that I've put her out by taking care of things on my own. And since we haven't eaten, we'll go there." Dylan laughed. "I have to take a shower. I run every morning if I get the chance but haven't lately since being in the operating room."

"Fine, I'll meet you there. Also, later we're going to meet with my mother-in-law. We usually don't meet in town, but I guess we're going Christmas shopping while the stores aren't busy. I myself order online whenever possible, but she claims it's much nicer to touch the things that you're buying first." Dylan snorted. "I couldn't care less if it felt as soft as it looked online. And if it didn't when I got it, I'd just send the shit back. I'll see you in a few."

15

The change of subject didn't bother her. Mildred, her scrub nurse, did it all the time. She'd be talking about cake and end up telling her about some shoes that she'd purchased.

Standing under the water made her moan. What a way to start out the day.

Ivy hoped that everyone else would be tolerant of her appetite — which was huge — as well as Meghan. Now that she'd put her in a pissy mood, she'd be that way all day. Washing her hair for the second time, Ivy smiled. This might be just what she needed to lighten her own mood.

As she was getting dressed, Ivy realized in that moment that this was literally the only clothing she had. Sitting down on the bed, Ivy felt sorry for herself for a little while before she got up to finish getting ready.

The insurance for her home was going to give her a nice settlement, not that she needed it. She hadn't had time to spend any money for ages, so it just sat in the bank. Ivy decided right then, she wasn't going to rebuild at all. Even though she had more than enough money to do that if she wanted, Ivy thought about the hassle of trying to find property to do that, filling the house when it was done, then moving in. She supposed that the latter would be easy enough. There wasn't anything left to be moved.

Going down the stairs, she saw that Meghan had waited. She, of course, was dressed like she was going to a wedding or something, while Ivy had on jeans and a T-shirt. Ivy's shoes, always a problem to her sister, were only tennis shoes and not heels. Ivy didn't know if after all this time she'd even be able to walk on the latter. Her opinion on the subject was that comfy was better than formal any day of the week.

"You certainly took your time about it. And you're paying for my breakfast. You should have told me that you had done it and I'd have not have had to stay up all night." Ivy pointed out that she'd not asked, and it was her home anyway, but Meghan said that it didn't matter.

"If it doesn't matter, then why do I have to pay for your meal?" Meghan huffed again, and Ivy laughed. "Oh, I forgot to tell you, I'm also having breakfast with Dylan."

Meghan stopped so suddenly that Ivy ran into her. Asking her what the hell she thought she was doing, her sister looked down at her outfit then back at her.

"Why didn't you tell me earlier, so I could have dressed up?" Ivy said that she didn't think she looked bad. "Of course, you don't. You wouldn't be caught wearing a dress for anything. When I pass away, the only thing that I'd like for you to do is wear a dress. Please?"

Ivy didn't even bother answering her. Going into the restaurant in front of her, Ivy realized that she didn't know any of the people around here at all. But thankfully, Meghan did. Making their way to the oversized table with the beautiful woman, Ivy did sort of feel like she should have taken better care for her appearance. Dylan introduced herself to her and Meghan sat down when Ivy did. Ivy just went with it. It was too late for regrets, as well as there was no other clothing that she owned.

Ivy ordered the big breakfast and asked for two of them. The woman taking their order didn't even bat an eye as she wrote it down. Ivy might like this area simply because they didn't get all twisted up about shit.

Chapter 2

Adam was going through seed catalogs when there was a knock at his front door. He put a sticky note to mark his place and made his way to the door just as Nate was coming from the kitchen with two maids he was training. He wasn't sure that was what they were called nowadays, so he kept his mouth shut and nodded. Adam let Nate open it while he stood behind it a bit.

"May I help you?" The woman there, what he could see of her between the doorjamb and wall, looked very pissed off. She told Nate she was looking for Adam. "I'm sorry, madam, but Lord Whitfield isn't at home at the moment. Would you like to leave a message for him?"

"No, I don't want to leave a fucking message, I want to find the bastard. He's going to take responsibility for his kid. I'm done with it." Adam could see the little boy then. He looked to be about twelve—way too old for him to have fathered him, even if that was possible. "Tell Adam Whitfield to get his ass in gear as well as his checkbook out. I'm suing him for back child support."

"And who shall I tell him is claiming to have had his child?" The woman told him she wasn't claiming anything, that the product was right there. She then told him her name. Adam leaned against the wall, glad now that Nate had opened it instead of him. "Ms. Crock — and the boy is?"

The name Crock? Adam didn't know a Crock. Crock of shit, yes, but not anyone else. When he looked through the split in the door and wall again, Adam saw her jerk the little boy's head up hard enough to make him cry out. Adam moved to stand in front of Nate, who was ready to fight for the boy, and she glared at him.

"Who the fuck are you? The bodyguard? You tell him that he's going to need one if he doesn't pay up." He told her that they had a video camera pointed right at her. With sound. "So the fuck what? Did you expect me to be afraid of that? I'm not. Now get your lord out here so I can give him his brat."

Adam stepped out onto the front porch. He looked up at the camera and then turned so that their entire conversation was recorded. Also, he wanted to see her reaction to what he was about to tell her. The little boy — Nathan, he'd heard — was terrified; he could almost taste it on his flesh. Adam did the only thing he could and moved little guy behind him and confronted his mother.

"I'm Adam Whitfield. The man who supposedly fathered this little boy." The woman paled just a little and backed up. "As you didn't even know who I was when you confronted my staff when you came to talk to me, I wonder how you're going to make it stick that I'm the father of Nathan. Because of the incapability of me fathering a child with you, I think that you should just go home before the police arrive."

"You're going to pay me." Adam just crossed his arms over his chest and stared at her. "That kid he's yours. I know it. You...

you got me drunk, and I didn't remember your face."

"Yes, I can see you getting drunk. You seem the type that would spend a great deal of time on a barstool. But you should know something else — you aren't taking the boy with you when you get the hell out of here." Adam glanced at young Nathan and saw something he was surprised to see — the naked look of someone that had a spark of hope. The sirens started to blare as they made their way up his driveway. "Too late for you, I'm afraid. The law is here."

By the time Sheriff Dale Winston got out of his cruiser, Ms. Crock had started screaming that Adam had stolen her child. Adam didn't say anything as she voiced the wrongs that had been done against her but waited to see where things ended up. Through the entire time that he was behind him, Nathan hadn't let go of the back of his shirt. And the grip was very tight too.

Dale shook his hand and told him that he was glad to see him. "Thank you, sir. How is your wife liking the area? I heard from my mom that she's already joined a few of the circles that she's in."

Dale laughed. "She sure has taken a liking to your parents. Why, your mom is about the sweetest person I've had the pleasure of meeting. And that dad and grandpa of yours? Well, they're just nice as punch on a summer day to us. I tell you, Adam, they're —"

"Are you fucking serious right now? Does this strike you as a social setting? In case you don't know, I'll tell you. No, it's fucking not." Dale stared at the woman with a cocked brow. Adam was sure that she wasn't giving up on this thing about him being the father of her child. "I want you to arrest him. For being a deadbeat dad. He's the father to my kid, and he either takes him, or pays —"

"I'll take him." That seemed to have knocked the wind

21

out of her sails, and she could only stare at him. "If that is my choice, then I'll gladly take him from you. Nathan, I want you to go into the house and find Mr. Turtle. Tell him that you'll need a room set up for yourself."

"Now you're going to kidnap my kid too? I would have thought that an upstanding man such as yourself would have just paid me off. And don't think I didn't notice that you took my kid. What the fuck sort of person are you? You can't have him." He pointed out that she'd given him to him as an ultimatum. Ms. Crock looked at the sheriff, and even he could see that she wasn't going to get any help from him. "I demand that you bring him into jail. I won't have him kidnapping my son, as well as being so far behind in child support that I have had to resort to other means of making money."

"And what sort of *other means* is that?" She stared at him when asked. "And where is Nathan when you're doing this *other means* thing? Surely, you're not taking him with you. I mean, such an upstanding person as you've shown us you are."

She was in over her head. Looking at Adam, then at Dale several times, she seemed confused, but no less pissed off. And when she opened her mouth, to no doubt blast him with more lies, he spoke before she could.

"I don't know what your game is here. I'm assuming you thought to make yourself a few extra bucks while you do whatever it is you've done before. But I don't think you want to fuck with me, Ms. Crock." She asked him why not, and even Dale laughed then. "Because I will most assuredly give in to my beast, which would like nothing better than to rip your fucking heart out and then tear you apart so that not even your own mother, should you have one, would be able to tell anyone what or who you were. Not even with dental records. Do I make myself perfectly clear? I hope so, for your own sake,

Shelby Crock, because I won't repeat myself. Now, be a good human and get the hell off my porch and out of my life, or so help me, you'll be dead before the sheriff here is able to put the cuffs on you."

She seemed to be waffling as to either what he was saying or whether she wanted to tangle with him. He, in a way, hoped that she would want to try her shit on him. Adam was as pissed off as he'd ever been before. Stretching his neck, he let a little of his cat run over him and she took a few steps back, right to the edge of the decking.

Adam was tempted to scare her so that she'd fall on her ass. But he only stood there, taking his own advice to remember that he was indeed being recorded. Laughing to himself, he moved back when Dale stepped in front of him. Apparently, he had no such illusions as to what the woman had been doing to him. Putting one hand on his gun and the other getting his cuffs out, the big man laughed.

"Now, I have it on good authority, Ms. Crock, that you've been trying this scam on several people of late. The rich and poor single men. The reason I know this is because I've had someone looking into this scam you have going." She opened her mouth and Dale simply put up his hand. "Don't say a word, not unless you want to spend a great many years in jail for kidnapping. That little guy in there? Well, he's been missing from his real family for a while now, hasn't he?"

"I have no idea what you're talking about." She looked around frantically now, her face tight with worry. Her hands were clasped in front of her, showing the whiteness of her knuckles as she stood there. Adam would not mess with Dale either.

The man was the biggest of the biggest bears. He had lived a hard life, having had his own sloth, a group of fellow shifters amounting to about four hundred, for more years than Adam had been alive. His dad could and would tell you tales about the man dating back for forty or fifty years.

Shelby was cuffed, and the boy was taken to the hospital. Nate traveled there with him in the cruiser, as they'd made fast and tight friends in the little time that they'd been together. Adam was glad that the boy was going to be returned to his real parents, but he couldn't help but wonder how that would fare for him. He'd been with that woman for a long time, and that could mess with the best of people. Even his parents might not see the same little boy they'd had when he was only a few months old.

Adam finished up the paperwork that he'd been working on, having fun with the batch of different seed companies that he'd gotten in the last few days. His mind drifted off and on to the child and the woman. Adam wondered how many others she'd pulled into her trap that made her think it was going to work on him. And how many other little kids had she taken to make it happen. He froze when Dylan touched his mind.

I was just talking to Dale. A great man, I think. Anyway, he said that he's made an arrest at your home. Are you all right? Should I be calling in favors? Or do I get to kick some ass for you? Either sounds like fun to me. He laughed with her, just as Nate put a plate of greens in front of him. The sun was setting earlier now, and he, like all shifters, needed more vitamins than he was eating this time of year. *By the way, have you heard the new doc is in town? Evan can't say anything but good news about her. I've met her as well as her sister. Believe it or not, Adam, they actually get along well.*

Are you giving me your itinerary for a reason? Because for the life of me, I have no idea why you'd care what I thought of your day. She laughed, and Adam found himself pushing the plate away and closing up his catalogs. He loved his sister-in-law more than he could explain. *Okay. Let's start over. You tell me what you want, and that will give me a chance to tell you no, I'm too busy. Then you'll disregard what I have to say about this by ordering me to do what you want.*

Okay, we're being blunt. I like that much better anyway. Since I've told you that there is a new doc, have you thought about her maybe being your mate? His stomach tensed up and he had to breathe in and out in order to think beyond what she'd just said to him. *By your silence, I'm guessing that you've not. There are two of them in town — sisters, as I've said. One is a surgeon. I've not told Evan just how good she is, but she's fucking damn good. Heart surgeon, with a great many praises in her portfolio. Right now, she has a license to practice here, but —* Adam, I can't hear you breathing. *You have to take in air or I'm going to have to come over there and make you breathe. Draw some air in then let it out. You can do it.*

Why would you say something like that? I mean, for all you know, she could be either Adrian or Blake's. She told him that they were next on her list to annoy about this. *You're enjoying this a little too much, if you ask me.*

I didn't, but if you want to know, it is sort of fun for me. Anyway, I had breakfast with her and her sister. She is human — nothing else that I've heard right now. Nice as fuck, and smart too if her colleagues aren't lying. Not as smart as I am, as you know, but right up there. He asked her again what this had to do with him, and he was reasonably sure that he knew the answer. *I want you to find her and end the suspense of this thing. Evan and I have a bet going on. He thinks that you're going to be an upstanding cat and go to her. I think, right now, that you're planning a fast getaway and you'll never return.*

While I still don't know why you're taunting me with this, I can tell you right off that I'm not the type that runs away. She said there was a first time for everything. *Certainly. But what kind of trouble*

25

do you think I'd be in if any of my other family found out what I was doing?

They'd hunt you down and have more fun than I'd be able to do to you. He said that she was correct. *All right. Come into town and sit in with me on a lunch meeting to make her stick around. According to Evan, she's run into some trouble. From what I've been able to gather, a guy from where she lived burned her house down because of something that went wrong in surgery with his son. Apparently, and I don't have all the details yet, there had been some kind of accident, and Ivy was in ER helping out when she declared his wife and daughters dead. The son — nineteen, by the way — had been driving, and was responsible for the accident. That's about all I know, other than that he died in surgery. Ivy was operating at the time. But I'll get more, you can count on that.*

I'm betting you will. What do you mean, someone burned down her home? She told him what she knew on that as well. *So, this man was pissed and decided the best way to deal with it was to do something as stupid as burning down her home?*

Get this — he even sent her a note signing his name to it. I don't know the man, but it sounds like — to me, anyway — he'd have blamed anyone that he could in his grief.

Adam also understood grief. When his grandma had passed, it had been hard on all of them. *All right. But I have no idea why you think that I can give you any help. And if she is my mate, meeting her under these circumstances isn't going to be helpful to any of us.* Dylan asked him why not. *Because, if I throw her onto the table and take her then, Mom is going to be pissed off at me about it. And I don't want that any more than I need a mate right now.*

Her laughter made him smile. Leaning over the catalogs that had arrived for him, Adam did more thinking than he did studying what he wanted. If she was his mate, he couldn't see how they could be more unsuited. A doctor and a farmer.

Christ, he'd be the laughingstock of the entire town.

~*~

Meghan was fidgeting again. Ivy was sure she burned up more energy doing that than Ivy did running daily. When she cleared her throat again, Meghan just glared at her and Ivy smiled.

"You'd not think this was so funny if you were trying to figure out what to do with your life right now." Ivy asked her sister what she meant. "I have no way of getting home, other than a flight. I don't have a driver's license, nor do I have anywhere near the money it would take to get me home in a cab. You are being asked to stay here, and I feel as if I've been tossed aside when this was all my idea."

"You're the one that decided for me to go to med school? Geesh, Meghan. If you have any more ideas like that, you might want to warn me. What if I had wanted to be a hobo or something? Riding the tracks and stealing from each little town I went through." Meghan glared harder. "You know that glaring at me doesn't work on me. I'm a doctor who gets those sorts of looks all the time. I do have some good news though. My new phone, with a different number, is to arrive today. It also has caller ID."

"Yes. And in the meantime, I have to put up with your stupid phone going off every ten seconds." Ivy asked her how that was possible she heard it with it being turned off. "Trust me when I tell you, I can feel it going off. How you can stand to have it off completely is beyond me. I would be lost without my phone."

"If I hadn't promised you and Evan that I'd have one, I'd not have bothered at all. But I am enjoying working with him. He's the kind of country doctor that I started out wanting to be." Ivy looked out the window of the little café that they were

27

having lunch in. "I might just leave the other one in your room in a place where you'd never find it but would hear it all the time."

"You would do something so mean, I know that."

Ivy watched the group coming toward the café. She knew who some of them were—others she could only guess were Whitfields as well. Whatever they wanted, it couldn't bode well for her or her sister. "I think we're about to have visitors. And whatever they want, it seems to be a family thing too."

Her sister pulled out her compact and looked in it to give the illusion that she wasn't concerned about anything. Ivy had to laugh at her. She loved her sister to the moon and back, but she sure was strange about whatever protocol she lived by in her head.

The people entered the café. They made the room, which was quite large, feel as if it had shrunk. She'd met one of the women earlier—Evan's wife, Dylan. A table was set up for them without them saying a word to anyone, and when they were seated, Dylan came to see them.

"We'd like to talk to you both." Before Ivy could decline their invite and leave, Meghan nodded and stood up. "Are you coming, Ivy, or should we all just try and crowd in this booth with you?"

"I'd like to see you try that." She stood up as well and was glad that she was taller than Dylan by a couple of inches. Not much, since the other woman seemed to exude confidence and readiness, but she'd take what she could. "I was just leaving."

Her food, which she'd ordered when she sat down, was put on the table she and Meghan were sitting at. Dylan smiled, a knowing one, and Ivy thought that she'd gladly have a smackdown with this woman. But she had a feeling that she'd never get in a single punch—the woman was just that good.

Dylan picked up Ivy's lunch—what she could, anyway—and made her way to the larger table. Meghan had a big shit eating grin on her face that had Ivy thinking that she had lost. Oh well, she'd come out on top if she had anything to do with it. But Ivy stopped moving when she saw someone she knew sitting with them.

Henry Cobb stood up when she was standing by the table. Ivy shook herself, thinking that this couldn't be the president of the United States having lunch with them. But as soon as he smiled, Ivy knew that it had to be him.

"Hello Ivy, Meghan. I'm glad to hear that you're going to be working with Evan. The man could use someone like you in his corner." Ivy told him that she wasn't working for anyone. "Oh really? Then why did I process your ability to practice here if that wasn't the case? Please, have a seat, my dear. I'm sure that the family here has a great many questions for us both."

Sitting down, she looked at the man at the end of the long table. He was staring at her like he recognized her. She didn't think that was possible, as she thought that she would have remembered someone that looked as yummy as he did. When Dylan laughed, everyone turned their attention to her—except the man. He continued to stare when Dylan was introducing everyone to her and her sister.

"Well, I did warn you of this." The man, his name was Adam, didn't bother looking at anyone else but her when he told Dylan to shut up. "This is epic. Welcome to the family, Ivy. I'm sure that you're going to make a wonderful addition to the rest of us."

Ivy wasn't sure what was going on, and frankly didn't care at this point. She had already decided to move on. The beach seemed to call for her. And the fact that she was going to retire from working unless she wanted to work was making the decision all that much better.

"I'm to understand that you and your sister have gotten this far on your way to the beach, Ivy. Were you planning to live there?" Ivy tore her eyes from the man to look at Henry. "I should probably explain how it is I know you. Even digging as deeply as Dylan can, I'm sure that she didn't find this. Go ahead, tell them how you know me."

"I was working in ER during my residency when there was a call about a man in an accident." She looked at Adam again. "Can you please stop staring at me like I hold all the secrets of your fucking life?"

"You're her. You're really her, aren't you?" Ivy looked at Adam and asked him what he was talking about. "I never thought that you'd be my mate when Dylan teased me about it. and to be honest, I thought you could do much better than someone like me. I'm just a farmer."

Henry laughed. "Yes, you're just a farmer, like I'm just running this country. Ivy, this is Adam Whitfield. He is a farmer as well as a rancher. He's very intelligent, strong minded, and he is a cat. A tiger—Bengal, as a matter of fact. And you, my dear, are his mate."

Ivy stood up when Adam did. She wasn't sure what to do, where to go. Glancing at her sister was no help—she was just staring at Adam like he was an all-day sucker and she was going to have at him. For some reason, that made her want to claw Meghan's eyes out. But she sat back down and picked up her fork, looking at her meal as she spoke about anything but what had just been said about Adam.

"I was finishing up my residency when there was an accident on the highway. I was living in Boston then, going to Harvard University for my last two years." Someone whistled, and she glanced at Evan as she continued. "I had won a full ride there, and was going to do the best I could be at being a doctor."

"And the accident that she's referring to is mine. I had been helping someone out, and we were headed out of town when another car didn't stop at a light and we were T-boned on the passenger side." Ivy looked at her sister then, knowing that she'd had no idea either as Henry continued, his voice low. "The woman, sadly, didn't make it—nor did the man who hit us. He was killed instantly. Jenny had internal bleeding that caused her to bleed out. I had several chest injuries, some of them severe, and my heart had been badly bruised in the process. Had it not been for the fast thinking of Doctor Walton here, I would have died as well. Or would have been on life support. Ivy saved my life."

"We'd been told that he was a John Doe, the woman Jane. I wasn't concerned as to who he was when they told me what had happened. I was more concerned that he was going to die. My professor asked me to operate on him, to help him live." Ivy glanced at Henry as she finished up. "Henry had just been nominated to take over the position of one of the congressmen for the state. Had anyone heard about the accident they would have thought it was foul play, no matter how much it was the other man's fault."

"So, it was kept out of the news. Why?" Henry told Sunny when she asked. "Were you the father of her child? I mean, you wouldn't be dating someone else's wife, would you?"

"No. I wasn't dating her. The newspapers were told that a man and his wife were killed, to keep them out of the loop about me taking Jenny to the airport to leave her husband." This time Carter asked why him. "Her husband was abusing not just her, but also his power in the House of Representatives. I was helping her to escape him when he was the one that hit us. He too was killed. So, in order to keep a scandal out of the paper, the accident was made to look like he and his wife had been out on a date. There was never any mention of me being anywhere near the place. They were out, a man hit them, and all died at the scene. End of story. At least that's what was reported to the news."

"Henry kept up with me. Would send me cards on my birthday and at Christmas. And when I was in town, he and I would have a nice dinner at his home until he became president. Then, because we didn't want the public to ask questions, we cut it off. All of it." Ivy stood up and pushed her chair in as she backed from the table. She looked at Adam. "I'm aware of what a mate is. But at this point, I'm not sure how much I can devote to a relationship. I've just lost my home and everything that was in it. I came here under false pretenses to help out Meghan, and we ran into trouble with my car. If it's all the same to you, I'm going to take the first flight out tomorrow morning to restart my life. I've devoted my entire life to becoming a good doctor. But now, I haven't any idea why I bothered."

Ivy left them there, even Adam, in favor of going on a run. Going to the bedroom she'd been using, Ivy put on her running shoes and her lightweight jacket and headed out of town, jogging and counting her footsteps so as not to think about anything else.

Chapter 3

Adam saw her before she saw him—or at least he had to think that was why she jogged on by him as he sat on the stoop of the B&B. Getting up and sitting on the rocker, so he could watch her the rest of the way into town, Adam wondered just how many miles a day she jogged. And why she did it.

Her form was beautiful. Ivy's body was toned so well that he wanted to see if all her muscles were that taut. While her hair was messily pulled into a ponytail, Adam thought that it wasn't because she was trying to be beautifully mussed, but that she simply didn't care what she looked like to others. He thought that was what made her more beautiful.

Adam tried to think of all the things that he'd heard about her. She was a surgeon, the best in her field. Hospitals across the world would call her up if she was needed. Ivy even taught a class or two at her local college, but only when she could devote her time to it. She didn't let anything interfere with her career.

Dylan had said that Ivy had money—enough for her to not work for the rest of her life and never stress about where her next meal was coming from. But Adam knew that she'd not do

33

that—quit—until she had no choice. Her feelings of obligation would keep her employed until she couldn't do it anymore. And even then, she'd be working at something. When she came up onto the porch where he was, she paused when she saw him there.

"I'm sorry about lunch." She just nodded, not saying or even giving anything away about what she was thinking. He decided right then and there that he'd never bluff with her. Her face was as unreadable as anyone he'd ever encountered. "I thought that we could talk, I just want to talk to you."

"For what reason? I'm well versed in what this means. I have plenty of friends that are shifters, and I know that this is a done deal for us. The only thing that I ask of you is that you don't interfere or try and make me quit what I'm doing." He didn't get a chance to answer her when she continued. "Recently I thought about it. Going to an island, lying on the beach all day, soaking up the sun. But I'd never be happy with that decision. I know that now."

"You do what you want. I'd never do that to you. I can understand having a passion about something." She was still standing near the steps and Adam was afraid that she'd take off again, and this time she might not return. "Could you come and sit with me?"

"I need to cool down." Adam sat, hoping that she'd give him at least a chance at this. "You should know that I'm not easy. I don't mean with sex, but with anything. I like my life just the way it is. I come and go as I please, and I do what I want. Even if I wanted to spend all my money on something foolish, that's my decision to make. I do not need a babysitter. I've been making choices for myself for a long time now."

"I agree with you. You've done well for yourself. Made a name for yourself in a profession that you seem to love. And

I like that you have a sister that you can depend on." Ivy told him that Meghan depended on her too much, but she loved her. "But she does want the best for you, I can tell that. I love my family as well. They're all I have, and I need them as much as I'm sure that you need Meghan."

Ivy came to where he was seated. Instead of sitting on the swing where he wanted her to be, she sat down on the chair as far away from him as she could get and still be on the porch. The fine dewiness of her sweat made him want to lick every inch of her. She glared at him, and he had a feeling that she had guessed what he was thinking.

"Dylan, she has this thing about investigating people that have anything to do with what she considers her family. I know a great deal of facts about you, but nothing about your personality. You said that you wanted to do things that you loved. I'd have it no other way. I farm, ranch too, and at the end of the seasons, I find that I wish for it all to do over. But I do enjoy the downtime I have too." She didn't say anything, but that was fine with him. "I have money—a great deal of it, as a matter of fact. We'll share that even if you decide to keep what you've earned for yourself."

"And you expect me to believe that?" Adam nodded, and she laughed, a short harsh one that made him think that she didn't believe him. "You'd just sign your possessions over to me without a question? As I said, I know shifters, and none of them willingly share with their other half. Many of the people that I worked with, they had hidden stashes all over the place. That isn't what I want from anyone. There is no mine and whoever's money or things. It's all in one pot that we both manage and share."

"I agree with you." He could tell that she still didn't believe him. "If you'd like, I can take you to the bank right now and have everything I own signed over to your name only."

"No. I'm not saying that." She looked away, and Adam could see the tears that filled her eyes. "I'm sorry. I'm being terribly selfish. I don't know what to do about this. I never thought to marry, have a mate, or even to have a friend with benefits. People are always out for more than they need. Meghan, to a point, is like that. But if I were to tell her no, and I do on a great many things, she'd not go behind my back to get it. Or try and convince me to give in."

"I'll never pressure you into anything. But I would like to be able to give you my opinion on things." She told him not to be an ass. Laughing, Adam felt better then. "I'm not. I promise you. And this is all new to me as well. I never thought...well, that's not true. I did think about having someone to love and cherish, much like my parents do. But I also knew that I'd never have a mate that would understand me."

"In what?" He told her, the best way that he could. "So, you think that a mate, in general, wouldn't like you for the simple reason that you're a man that enjoys menial labor. Having the earth give you as much as you put into it is the most noble job that I can think of. You give, I'm betting, as much as you get from it."

"True. I do that. But also, I have never thought that what I do means as much to anyone else as it does to me. Having you as my mate, my other half—it never occurred to me that I'd meet someone like you, a person that shares, while not the same work as me, a job that you enjoy as much as I do mine." Adam thought that he was not only understanding her but shared her heartbreak as well as a passion for what they did. "Ivy, I will tell you, on my mother's heart, I will never ask you to do something that I'd not do myself."

When she looked away and out to the street, he did as

well. Watching the couple walking along with the small child between them while they argued made him feel sorry for their daughter. When they let her hand go to argue more, Adam watched the couple.

When Ivy stood up, Adam did as well. The tension in her body was almost palpable, like he could touch it. Leaping over the railing, Adam saw the car speeding toward the child as soon as Ivy ran into the street and grabbed the little girl.

It was over in seconds. The little girl was cradled in Ivy's arms even as the car careened off the street and toward the couple on the sidewalk. Adam watched, in horrific detail, as the woman was hit by the runaway car and the man tossed over the top like a rag doll.

Evan, come to Main Street now.

Without question, his brother said that he was on his way. Adam made sure that Ivy and the child were safe before he went to the couple. The man was dead. The woman, pinned between the car and the building behind her, was talking to Ivy. Adam approached them slowly, not sure what he was going to see.

"Call an ambulance." He pulled out his cell phone to make the call. Ivy was already working with the woman to ascertain what had happened to her body. "My name is Doctor Walton. I'm going to have the driver back up. I'm going to help you. But you'll be in more pain. Let it take you under, all right?"

The driver was out, his airbag deployed. Ivy asked Adam to back up slowly, like snail slow. Adam was able to reach into the car and put it in reverse to do what she asked. When the woman screamed and slumped across the hood of the car, Ivy got on the crushed hood of it and held onto the woman.

When the car was moved enough for Ivy to work, she did what came to her as naturally as breathing did to him. She was looking over the woman when Adam asked her if he could do anything to help.

"I need my bag. It's in my room on the floor of the closet. Please bring it to me as quickly as you can."

He turned to run to the B&B when he saw Michael, son to the owner of the place, rushing toward them with the black bag in his hand. "Thank you very much. Is the ambulance on its way?"

Michael said that he'd called it in. Adam told her that his brother was on his way too. Nodding, Ivy dumped out her bag of tricks, what Evan called his, and he watched her pick up what she needed without missing a beat.

The woman was unconscious but still screaming out when she was in pain. Ivy spoke to her, even though she wasn't answering her. She told her that she had her, that she was working as best she could and needed for her to fight. Adam looked over at the dead man, the one that she'd been arguing with, and saw his brother, Blake, was talking to the little girl. She'd been unharmed, it seemed to him, and he was glad for that.

By the time Evan and the ambulance showed up, Ivy had the woman somewhat stable. An IV was running, and the worst of her wounds were covered with gauze. She was still bleeding, of course, but Ivy never stopped reassuring her that she had her. Ivy was working on setting her leg so that she could be moved onto the gurney to take to the hospital.

When she stood up, letting Evan move to where she was, Adam saw that she was covered in blood. Her shirt had taken the worst of it, and her shoes had been covered in it as well. Evan was barking orders to the medics as Ivy headed to the man that had been with the woman.

His neck had been broken if the way his head was laying was any indication. His left arm had a bone protruding out from his flesh. The wounds on his face looked like road rash, like when a person hit the pavement during a bike crash. His eyes were open, and that gave Adam the willies.

Pronouncing the man dead seemed to have been unnecessary, but as soon as he thought that, he realized why she'd done it. No one would waste time on trying to bring him back and would be able to work on those that had a chance.

As the man was being loaded up in the first of two ambulances, he asked Ivy again if she needed anything. Shaking her head, she sat on the sidewalk and watched Evan. He looked at him too, wondering why anyone would think that what she'd just done for this family was anything short of a miracle. She had more than likely saved the woman's life, and the child's for sure. And in that moment, Adam fell in love with his mate. Ivy was perfect as far as he was concerned, and if he had to work on it for their entire lives, he was going to make her realize that as well.

~*~

Ivy was lead surgeon on this one, and Evan was assisting her. As she scrubbed in, she wondered at the stupidity of people. The man that had hit the family had been drinking, driving, and texting when he'd hit them. And even though there were cautions as well as commercials on television and the news about doing this, he'd still managed to kill one person and critically injure another.

"Are you all right?" She looked at Evan and asked him what he meant. "Honey, I don't know if you realize this or not, but you talk to yourself. Others, humans I mean, might not hear it, but I have excellent hearing. So again, are you all right?"

"I don't know, to be honest." The scrub nurse came to help her gown up, and she was startled to see that it was Mildred, the one she'd been working with since she'd begun working as

39

a surgeon at the other hospital. "Where did you come from? I thought you were set to retire soon."

"That man there, he talked me into it." She grinned at Ivy as she helped her into her gown and mask. "He thought that you could use someone in your corner. I was only too happy to come be with you again. Retirement ain't what I thought it would be."

"I thought that you could use something familiar to help you work. I know that I need something like that as well. Beethoven is my way to concentrate better." Evan smiled at her through his mask. "She wasn't hard to convince anyway."

"No. I should have made him promise me the world. But I have to tell you, Ivy, it was my greatest pleasure to be working with one of the best there is." Ivy wanted to hug her, but then they'd have to start all over with prep. Instead, she walked into the operating room with a lighter heart, and happiness beyond what she thought she should feel for what she was doing.

Ivy didn't know what to say to Evan. He'd done something really nice for her, without bragging about what he'd done or asking for anything in return. She had to turn away from them both, she was so overwhelmed.

The operating room was large, much more so than most of the bigger hospitals had. When the woman — another thing that she strived for was not to know patient's names — but when she was wheeled into the room with them, Ivy had a small feeling of fear. It took her several seconds to gain control of her emotions and start working. Once she was in the mindset, Ivy moved toward the table and began to work.

The surgery took almost five hours. By the time she stepped back, Ivy felt as if she'd been wrung out and hung out to dry. As soon as she left the room, Ivy made her way to the bathroom. Another thing that she did with nearly every operation was go to the bathroom and throw up. She wasn't sure where the habit had formed, and it was something that drained her as well. This time, however, was different. Not only did she not feel the urge to toss her cookies, but she felt better knowing that she'd done all that she could.

When she came out of the ladies' room, both Adam and Evan were there. She didn't know what to say to the second and wasn't sure why Adam was there. Ignoring them both, she talked to Mildred about what she wanted, and waited in the scrub room long enough to get her bearings back. Going back into the hallway again, she saw that now there was only Adam. She asked him where Evan had gone.

"I think he's in post op. Even when he's not in charge with a patient, he goes to check on them. He said that it covers his ass. I have no idea what would make him worried. He's been doing this since he graduated from med school." Nodding at Adam, she told him that she had to shower and change. "I thought as much. I'll be waiting here for you. I'd like to take you to dinner. It's been a long and stressful day for you, and I've asked the police to wait until you've unwound. I know I had to after we left the scene. By the way, Evan said that she was going to make it, thanks wholly to you."

"I doubt that he was serious." Adam told her that as far as he knew, Evan had never said anything like that about another doctor he worked with. "I'm sure that he didn't think that I could have done that without him. He was a great deal of help." Adam didn't try and convince her otherwise.

Ivy headed to the doctors' showers and stood under the spray as soon as she'd discarded her scrubs. She'd have to wear another pair home, as her clothing was covered in blood. But the water was hot and plentiful—something else that bigger hospitals didn't have. There was no valve that would only give you ten minutes of water, or tepid water that would freeze you before you were finished cleaning up.

When Ivy joined Adam and his family in the waiting room, Evan asked her if they could come to dinner with them. She really didn't want to go but glanced at Adam for his answer. Ivy noticed that Meghan was with them as well, and she looked too hopeful to not say she didn't care. Adam said that he'd love for them to all be there, but it was entirely up to her. Ivy nodded and then realized how hungry she really was.

They were seated in a room by themselves and she thought for sure that they were getting special treatment, and that embarrassed her. But Ivy soon realized it was because they were loud. Not just shouting, but their laughter as well as the teasing of each other. Ollie, Adam's grandfather, sat beside her, and Adam across from her.

"I heard you did a fantastic job in there. You saved that woman and her little girl." Ivy asked him how the child was. "Faring well. She's a mite on the frightened side—I guess that car was coming right at her when you stepped in."

"Yes, well, her parents had neglected to keep an eye on her when they were arguing." Ollie told her that he was seeing that more and more, where no one was paying attention to their surroundings, and it was scary. "I know that it was nutty to leap in front of that car like I did, but I just couldn't see her getting harmed. I had no idea that her parents would be hit. Not that I would have done it differently, but she wasn't going to be hurt. Not if I could do something about it."

"Of course not. And a right good job of it you done too." Ivy was charmed by the elderly man. He was sweet, compassionate, and smarter than he let anyone believe that he was. "Have they convinced you to hang around yet? I'm telling you now that if you leave, Adam will be following you, and me too. I love those boys a great deal, but Adam, he had a special place in my wife's heart, and mine too. I love them all, like I said, but he makes me think of my wife who passed."

"I'm sorry about your loss. It's difficult when you lose a loved one. My parents have been out of mine and my sister's life for a very long time. And sadly, we like it that way. They both have been married and divorced so many times, that it was a nightmare for us to try and keep up with the children they each had. Or got with another marriage." He told her that she must have been a wee baby when they divorced. "I wasn't very young. I mean, I was sixteen when they were already married a couple of times. Meghan came to live with me and keep me sane, so I could finish up college. I'd been taking classes there and at high school at the same time. I was working my way through my residency before I finally understood they didn't leave us but wanted a lifestyle that wasn't the norm. Whatever that might be, I guess. I hope they're having a good time, at whatever they're doing now."

"What a wonderful thing to say. I bet they'd be very proud of their girls." Ivy said that it didn't really matter and looked over at her sister. "She's smart too, I think, but doesn't use it much. I'm not saying that she's dumb or anything but I think that she just doesn't care."

"No, she cares, but not in the way that most do. Meghan is stylish, has a perfect smile, a laugh that makes those around her smile. Not that she does that for attention, but she cares about how she is perceived." Ivy laughed a little. "I'm the one that doesn't care. I couldn't care less if I have lipstick on, I don't even wear it when dressing up. If my hair is messy, I just resort to pulling it into a ponytail. I've not worn heels since I graduated from college. And only then because it was a requirement. No, Meghan cares about appearances. But I really don't know why she worries — she's very beautiful."

"And you think that you're not?" She looked around the table before she answered him. "You can't believe that, darling. You're the most beautiful creature I've ever seen."

"Creature?" He told her that they were all creatures when you were a shifter. "Oh. Okay, I get it. But no, I've no delusions about what I look like."

"That's wonderful, but I think that you're beautiful." Adam took her hand into his when he commented on what they'd been talking about. Ollie made excuses about speaking to his son. They were a tight family, so she didn't have any trouble believing that he really wanted a conversation with Oliver. "Are you all right now?"

"I think so. Thanks for asking." He nodded and asked if he could hold her hand. "All right, but I don't have silky hands. Mine are callused and strong. I have to keep them nimble so that I can operate."

"I think that they're perfect. And you can see by my hands that I'm just as callused and nimble. Just a few weeks ago, I was rolling hay for the winter and making sure that I had all the equipment put away until spring." He kissed the back of her hand and looked at her. "I have never seen eyes the color of yours. I've been trying since I met you to figure out what color they are. And I love the color of your hair as well. Flaming red, my mom called it."

"My driver's license says red. I don't think there was a choice for flaming." He laughed, and she felt herself relax more. "As for my eyes, they're also marked as mundane green, though I was told once that there are emeralds out there that pale in comparison. I think my dad said that to me before."

"Well, I don't think he could have been righter." Their dinner was placed in front of them and she saw that he had an appetite as large as hers. The only difference was, he was a shifter that needed to fill his other needs, and she just burned calories like it was her job. "I'm glad to see that you eat well. I'm not trying to insult you, I promise, but I was watching what your sister ordered. She is sort of finicky, isn't she?"

Ivy looked at the plate in front of Meghan. There was a salad with no dressing, a glass of water with a lemon in it, as well as no rolls or bread of any kind. She knew that Meghan wouldn't have dessert, nor would she snack later. Her sister had a very strict diet that she watched. Ivy ate what she wanted when she wanted and didn't care who said anything. Ivy hadn't gained an ounce in ten years and wouldn't have cared if she had.

Eating was fun with Adam talking to her. She wasn't sure that she could have gotten used to it, having such a loud group around her, but for now, it was all right. When the dessert cart was rolled into the room as soon as they were finished, Ivy took the only thing that she loved more than ice cream—key lime pie with whipped topping. Adam chose lemon meringue pie, another favorite of hers.

Ivy opted to walk home from the restaurant. It wasn't that far, and she needed to unwind for a little while. She was on call through the night with their patient, and that sort of made for a sleepless night. Adam walked with her. She wasn't sure what he was going to expect when they got there, but she did allow him to hold her hand.

"I've got things coming to the house tomorrow and the next. I bought my grandda's house when he moved in with my mom and dad." Ivy didn't know where he was going with this, so said nothing. "I was wondering if you'd like to come over, see the house, as well as tell me what you think of what I chose. I've never been much of a shopper, so I had no idea what to order."

"I'm sure that it's fine." He nodded, then shook his head. "I don't understand. Did you order something that you know that you're going to hate?"

"No, it's not that. I would like for you to tell me what you want in a house. You don't have to move in with me, though I'd not mind that, but I would like for you to give me your opinion. I loved sitting in my grandda's chair, but it had a spring in it that would catch me off guard if I wasn't paying attention." She laughed when he did. "I think I might still have a couple of bruises from it. I know that you've recently lost your home and contents. So, I would also like to take you ornament shopping. I've decided to have a tree this year, and I have very few decorations, not counting the ones that my mom has given all of us."

"To be honest with you, Adam, I've not put up a tree for a long time. I'm rarely home, and when I am, I just flop on the bed until I have to go to work." Shaking her head, she thought about the call she'd gotten from Lily Danger — suitably named — her old boss. "Right now, my former boss is putting me on the schedule to work there, when I've told her numerous times that I'm on vacation. I think she feels that she can bully me into it. And since that doesn't work, she's pulled out the big guns and told me that patients would die because I didn't come in when I was needed."

"She sounds like a person who is used to getting their way." Ivy told him that he had no idea. "What are you going to do about it? I will do whatever you want, move back or stay here. I just want to be where you are."

"I don't know, to be honest. I love working with Evan. He's brilliant but not pushy. And he's not opposed to giving me the lead when he thinks I can do a better job." Ivy laughed. "I'm not sure why he thinks that; other than me being a heart specialist, he's as good if not better than anyone I know. Including myself."

"I don't think he sees it that way. And Evan has always been like that. He was never one to make his point by running over someone else." She looked at the door, then back at him. "I guess I should make my way home. If you want to come over tomorrow, I can send a car for you. Or I can come into town, we can have breakfast with you, and take you there. I'm pretty flexible until eleven, when they're scheduled to deliver."

"I'd like that. But don't expect me to have any opinions on your home, Adam. I'm taking this one day at a time. I need to do that." Adam told her that he understood, and she believed him. "Okay, I'll meet you at the restaurant and then go to your home. I'll see you tomorrow."

When he walked away, leaving her there, she nearly called him back, to have someone to talk to that didn't need her to agree with everything they had to say. And to be able to talk about work or what had happened to whomever she was working on. She loved her sister very much, but Meghan hated her talking about work. And she wasn't happy when Ivy was leaving in the middle of the night or when they had plans. Adam was comfortable.

Going into the widened hall that served as the check-in desk, Ivy made her way up to her room rather than sit with her sister in the dining area drinking tea. Suddenly she was exhausted.

Chapter 4

Adam watched Ivy cross the street to where he was. She was wearing her jogging clothes, and he wondered if she had already been out or she was headed for a run after this. When she smiled as she sat down, Adam could have gladly danced a jig around the room.

"I'm sorry I'm late." Adam told her that he'd not noticed. "I'm sure you've been sitting here thinking that I stood you up. But I got sidetracked before leaving my room, and I just finally had to hang up so that I could get out in time to meet you. What are you having?"

Adam laughed while she placed her order first. She was a good hearty eater, but you'd not think that to look at her. She was slim, tall, and toned. After ordering his own breakfast, he took her hand into his.

"It was your boss again, wasn't it?" She nodded and polished off a large glass of grapefruit juice and asked for another. "What was she doing this time? Begging you to come home again?"

"Lily doesn't beg. She just assumes that you're going to do

what she wants with everything. I never have, so I'm not sure why she thinks this will work on me. But now that I'm nearing the end of my vacation time, I've decided to see if your brother will let me be a partner with him in his practice. I don't want you to ask him—I'm not fishing for you to do that. But I would like to know if you think he'd partner with me."

"I'm sure that he'll drop to his knees and beg you to come work with him. He was telling me a few weeks ago that he hated having to send patients to the bigger hospital in Columbus. Evan is one of those doctors that loves to be a part of the lives of the people that he sees. Not nosey, but I think he could name every baby he has delivered and each patient that has died while in his care. Which, you might want to know, is very few."

"I thought that too. I love that he's put that big pin board up with all the babies that he's brought into the world. He has a great deal of pride when he shows it off." Adam watched her face as she talked about Evan and what he had accomplished since moving back home again. "I don't think he would have been able to do that working for someone else. He told me a little about why he moved back home."

"Yes. I think he did it more for Dad than he did anyone else. Then once he was here, I think he realized how much he hated working so far away. And Grandda has come out of his funk since we've all bought houses and are putting down roots to stay nearby. Mom loves that, especially." Ivy told him that she'd not known her grandparents since they were both gone before she'd been born. "I miss my grandma every day. She was the rock in this family. Not that my mom wasn't too. But we all knew that Grandma was the one that ran the roost, so to speak."

Their breakfast came just as he was telling her about his house. It was a place of memories for him, and an accomplishment too. "The kitchen was redone just before my grandma passed away. She really loved to cook, but especially bake. Her cookie jars weren't just for show, but they were always full of some kind of treat." Ivy buttered a fresh hot biscuit as he spoke. "We have nine bedrooms. That was a lot even back when Grandda had the house built. None of us, when we were younger, would have missed out on a chance to spend the night with them. It was wonderful because they spoiled us just enough."

"Nine bedrooms? Sheesh, you're not planning on me filling them all, I hope." He nearly choked on his tea when she laughed too. "I've been giving things around my life a lot of thought since last night. I want to be your mate, but I don't want you to rush me into sex. I'm not very good at it anyway."

"Why would you say that?" She shrugged, and he smiled. "Oh no, you're not getting off that easily. Tell me why you think that you're not any good at sex. Because if someone else told you that, they need to be shot. Just looking at you makes me hard."

He'd not meant to say that to her, and she was just as surprised if the way her spoon was paused before reaching her mouth was any indication. When she put down the utensil, he told her that he was sorry. She nodded before speaking again.

"I'm not good at it. I mean, yes, I've been told that from a couple of lovers that I had. I was too boring. Or selfish, and that one surprised me. I was only selfish because the guy was finished way before I was even close." Her face brightened up with embarrassment. "I can't believe I'm telling you this."

"It's all right. But if you'd share the guy's name that said that to you, I can go and teach him a few manners." She laughed, and he joined her. Ivy clearly believed what had been said to her. "I promise not to rush you into making love with me. But I'm not promising that I won't want to touch you, to be with you as closely as I can. You mean the world to me, Ivy, even though we've only known each other for a few days."

Picking up her fork again, she played with the sausage gravy that was smothering the fluffiest biscuits he'd ever eaten. Of course Adam would never tell his mom that. Hers were delicious too, but there was something about Milly's that made his mouth water just thinking about them.

"I don't know what I'm doing. I mean, whenever I'm near you, I feel so calmed by you. I don't feel like I'm failing at life. I know that I should be on top of the world — being a doctor is all I ever wanted. But it hasn't been that fulfilling for a long time. I think coming here with my sister, even under false pretenses, was the best thing I needed. For myself." She looked at him and he could see the worry in her eyes. "If your brother doesn't agree with taking me on, I am seriously thinking of quitting what I'm doing. I never realized how much I wasn't happy with my work until Evan showed me how much he loved what he was doing."

"At one time, Evan was like you are now — torn between coming home to live out the rest of his days or going to a job that didn't do anything for him. Evan spoke to me about it before Dylan came into his life. He was right where you are now, indecisive as well as bored." He took her hand. "I don't think you have to worry about him not wanting to work with you. All he's talked about since you two were in surgery together is how much he admired you and what you did."

Adam reached for his brother and told him what was going on with Ivy. Evan was so quiet for a while that Adam was sure that he'd been someplace where he couldn't reach him. But he asked where they were right now.

If you're coming here just to talk to her, you're going to mess up the progress that I've made with having her trust me. I mean, she's not begging for me to ask you – in fact, she said not to. But I think that she needs this as much as you did at one time. Evan said that he was coming in for breakfast with Dylan, and that would be his cover. *Good. And remember, I didn't speak to you at all. All right? I don't want her not to trust me.*

This would be the only time I think you should do this, going behind her back. I understand what you're doing now, I do, but don't make a habit of it. Women are pretty nasty when they think that you're trying to take over their lives. Not that you are, but she might think that. Adam asked if he'd done that to Dylan. *Yes. Just the one time, and never again. I promised her.*

Evan and Dylan were arguing when they came into the place. It was an ongoing tiff with them that Dylan hated bacon – liked the smell but didn't care for the taste of it. Evan didn't really care for it either, but he wanted to make Dylan pissy for some reason. Adam thought that his brothers were all saps in the way they treated their mates and wondered if he'd do the same thing. Adam turned and looked at Ivy and realized that he was already being a sap. Who knew that it could feel so good to be labeled as such?

Dylan stomped off and came and sat at their table. Adam laughed. She was holding in her laughter, and Adam realized that she was making Evan pissy for the same reason. As soon as she sat down with Ivy, Evan had him crushed against the window by sitting with him.

"She is driving me nuts." Ivy laughed at Evan and he smiled at her. "You're up bright and early. I hope you weren't called last night. As far as I thought, it was a quiet night."

"It was. I'm usually up by this time anyway since I run about five miles before I allow myself to shower." Dylan asked her why she did something so strenuous first thing in the morning. "It loosens me up. Burns off whatever stress I might have going on and such." Ivy looked at Adam. "Sometimes the stressors aren't anything but my own mind making things look a great deal worse than they really are."

Adam knew that she was talking to him, but what she meant was nothing he understood. But before Adam could ask her, Evan and Dylan ordered their food while continuing to argue over the bacon issue. It wasn't until they were all served that Evan started talking to Ivy.

"How much longer do you have on your vacation? I mean, it can't be that much longer, is it?" Ivy told him that she'd not decided as yet. "I don't understand. Are you planning to not go back home? Because if that's your plan, I would love to talk to you about being partners. You have no idea how much I've enjoyed having you around and having someone to help with surgeries as well as patient calls. I'd gladly sign a partnership with you today."

"I'm not sure." She played with her food without looking at anyone. "I'm already on the schedule at the other hospital. In fact, she has put me on it for tomorrow. I still have two weeks left, but Lily doesn't like to be told no. Or she simply thinks that I'm going to drop everything and come running back by blackmailing me with patients dying. Or that is what she is going to tell those that need me."

"She needs to have the shit knocked out of her."

Adam had to agree with Dylan. The woman had been calling the B&B so much that he'd asked to have the calls forwarded to their home. And from there, they were put off by the staff. Nate had enjoyed, just a little too much, telling the woman that Ivy wasn't home. Then this morning when she'd gotten up to leave, a courier had brought a certified letter to the B&B where Ivy and Meghan had been staying.

"I really don't think that I want to go back. But I have a

feeling that things are not going to be that much better here."
Adam asked her why not. "I don't know what to do about the
two of us. I mean, I really like being with you, and your family.
But I'm still trying to think about what I'm supposed to do with
everything else."

"There isn't anything that we can't deal with here or there."
Adam told her that he'd go with her, no matter where it was, if
she'd only say the word. "I cannot be without you, Ivy. You're
my life. And as much as I'd like to tell you that I'd rather not
move from my family, I don't want to leave you twice that
much."

"You see, that's not helping me." He grinned at her. "You're
not as charming as you think when you do that."

"They all do it. I think it's something that they learned from
Ollie. He's a charmer from way back." Ivy smiled at Dylan when
she reached for the last biscuit in the basket. "I'm to understand
that you've hired a staff. It's about time, if you ask me. That
house is much too large for you to wipe up after yourself. By
the way, I heard that you guys had furniture now. Thank God.
I hated that chair with the nasty spring. I think that I could use
it as a torture method. I think I could get some good intel by
using it."

No more was said about the partnership. Adam knew that
she was thinking hard on it. He was proud of Evan for not
being his usual pushy self. He supposed that Dylan had told
him what to do. Adam thought that he'd do the same — wait for
her to bring it up again and let her make the decision. But this
thing with Lily was going to stop soon. She was stressing out
Ivy too much.

"Did you read over the letter that came from Mercy
Hospital?" Ivy nodded and handed it to him. He hadn't looked
at it — without her trusting him, he'd not do that to her. Instead

of reading it over, like was his intent, Dylan asked for it and he gave it to her. "Nate said that she calls the house no less than five or six times a day. What makes her think that all this that she's doing to you is going to help you in your decision?"

"I have no idea. It's not like it's worked before. And you should hear her bitch and complain when I have to go to another hospital to work. You'd think that I was her kid and had run away from home. Then there is the added pain in the ass about her crying when she doesn't get her way." Dylan laid the letter down and looked at Ivy before speaking. "What is it?"

"You can sue her." Ivy asked her how she'd come to that conclusion. "Well, first of all, she's harassing you. Not just by her wanting you to cut your earned vacation short, but she's calling your household several times a day. I'd have Nate keep track of the future calls with times and dates in the future. From there, I have an attorney that can make her wish that she'd held up her end of the bargain."

"I'm game." Adam was surprised that Ivy had given in so quickly. She must have really been stressing about this. "What is it I have to do?"

"You let me make a few phone calls and I can have it taken care of." Ivy asked her if this was because they wanted her to work for them and Dylan smiled. "You're scary when you look like that. I'm sure you know that, but I'm almost afraid to find out what your plan is."

"No, I'd do this anyway. I love making people piss themselves. Also, and this is the real kicker, she is going to owe you an apology—a big one—when I'm finished with her." Ivy said that if she could make this go away, then she'd stay. "That's really not why I'm doing this."

"I know. There is something else you should be aware of. I have two more years left on my contract with the hospital. Then

I'm sort of a free agent. Do you think you could get that off my back as well?" Dylan didn't answer verbally, but she did smile. "Thanks. And I'm serious, if you can get me out of the contract as well as get Lily off my back, I'm here to stay."

Adam would take what he could with this. Ivy was staying because of the offer of help with her boss. He could have been pissy, he supposed, pointing out that he had promised her the world. But he didn't. She was staying, and that, to him, was the most important thing.

~*~

Adrian was glad to be doing this for his family. He'd only just taken a few refresher courses to fatten his package when it was time for the voters this fall. And it would help him a great deal if he was to make it as president. Adrian knew that he had a long way to go with his plan, but he was happier more to be helping Ivy. She had taken a great deal of his heart since being here.

When he was called into the office of the president of the hospital, Adrian went in with his notes all in line, Dylan standing by if he needed her, as well as having witness facts to go with the rest of what he was doing. Taking a seat when it was offered, Adrian wasn't the least bit surprised to see that there was more than just the president. It looked as if the entire board was there. Adrian didn't waste any time and got right to why he was there.

"Lilian Jane Donaldson has been harassing my client, who is also to be my sister-in-law soon. Here you will find the number of calls that she's made to her home. There are couriers coming by their home almost daily as well, trying to blackmail her into coming back to work." He handed the list to each man, glad now that he'd taken the time to make copies of what he had. "Doctor Ivy Walton applied for her vacation time within the parameters of the agreement that she has with this hospital. Giving notification of her time away from work, Ivy—Dr. Walton—had it all approved to be away for several weeks. It just so happened that she met my brother and decided to give her notice to coincide with her vacation time, giving plenty of time for a replacement to be found."

He watched as each man looked through the things that he'd given them. They were quiet for the most part, leaning in to talk to each other. Adrian had a feeling that they'd not known of this development, nor the fact that their biggest moneymaker had had to resort to bringing in a lawyer to take care of her troubles.

"Ivy has been a great asset to this hospital. Her revenue alone has made it so that we could run a highly rated facility." Adrian said nothing, not even to smile at them when he knew that Lily hadn't shared any of Ivy's issues with the board. "If you don't mind me asking, why did she not come and talk to us? I think we could've worked something out. We'd even be willing to give her an increase in her pay. And more vacation time."

"It is well past that, I'm afraid. As you can see by the attachments to the first sheet of grievances against Miss Donaldson, several other doctors, as well as nurses, have left because of run-ins with her. Several doctors that I've spoken with were told that going to the board, above Miss Donaldson's head, would result in lost overtime. Nor would their insurance be paid and written write ups would be filed on small infractions that did not warrant them. Actions that were not only made up, but unlikely to have been done by any of the doctors."

Adrian handed them each some of the things that he'd found in files on the doctors. Not only were their names there to accompany them, but also the doctors' signatures and phone numbers, in the event that they'd like to get in touch with them.

Hey, I just found out some juicy information that might seal the deal on this broad. Little Miss Lily has been taking the bonuses for all the doctors. Not only that, but anytime there's an award dinner or a yearly meet and greet, she's made sure that none of them are able to attend. And barring that, she's kept it from them so that she could take all the kudos when they were given to them. Adrian asked Sunny how she'd found this out. *You don't want to know. But suffice it to say, the shit is going to hit the fan in about ten minutes. I've had it explained to the few doctors that are left here, which is way less than they had when Ivy was working. They are, needless to say, pretty pissed off about it.*

Are you telling me that they're on their way here? Sunny laughed. *Christ, this is going to be epic. I'm glad that I got to be a part of this. Ivy will be hanging around now, and Adam will be able to be with us. I have to tell you, Sunny, I was terrified that they were going to move away.*

Me too. I really like her. She's all soft and mushy about some stuff, but a real bear when it comes to things being right and equal. I'm going to have so much fun with her when they're married. She laughed. *I'm hoping they bond soon. I sort of feel sorry for your brother.*

Yeah, I do as well. But he is doing what he thinks is right with her. She strikes me as someone that hides her emotions inside, and when it blows over, someone will be picking up the pieces for a very long time. And her feelings for Adam, I think, are terrifying her. Something that she's never felt before, and it's taking over. Sunny said that's what she'd thought as well. *Hmm. Sunny, they're here.*

It had never occurred to him that his grandda was part of the board at this hospital too. His mom and dad were on the one at home, but he'd never thought to even ask about this one in Columbus. His grandda was leading the pack, so to speak, when about a dozen men and women came into the room.

"What's the meaning of this, Mr. Whitfield? You show up now, with these people, instead of sitting with the board? I won't have it." Grandda sat down and winked at Adrian before turning to the four men in the room. "Mr. Whitfield, can you please tell me what this is all about?"

"I can. I can. But I think these people are going to tell you in their own words. There is some nasty stuff going on around here, and they're here to let you know just how disappointed they are in the lot of you." The eldest man stood up then sat down when Grandda snapped at him to do so. "You've been mighty negligent around here, Bob. You've went and lost you about the best there is in the surgical field, not counting my grandson. And on top of that, these people here have been deprived of their money and awards. That woman, Miss Lily, has made a mess of things, and now, since you didn't step in when you should have, you're about to see the back end of the turkey as it goes over the fence when it comes to keeping this place running."

"Mr. Whitfield, we've only been made aware of this today." Grandda told him that he was a liar and he should have noticed that they were losing doctors and other staff right and left. "We assumed that things were going well. No one came to us about any of this."

"As he said, you are a liar." The doctor that was standing next to the wall handed Adrian several pieces of paper. "You'll see there that not only have I made several complaints about lost wages, no pay raises, as well as lost vacation time, I've emailed the board and sent out notices of the way things are headed. And all to no avail. You'll also find in those papers my resignation. I can't work under these conditions. And I don't think any of us will."

The table was flooded with unfinished paperwork that had been due weeks after the man had demanded someone else do it—resignations. Notices of strikes, as well as disciplinary actions taken against the employees that were not just untrue but unfounded as well. Adrian just sat back and let the men hang themselves. There was just too much evidence on what had been right under their noses. His cell phone was ringing just as the second man in line began telling them what he'd been putting up with. It was Henry Cobb.

"Are you trying to kick me to the curb before my time here is up?" Adrian laughed when he did. "You've done a good job with this. This is going to be another feather in your cap when this comes out in the paper. And there isn't any way for them to shove this under the rug now."

"They're claiming that they'd not known anything about this. But that's been quashed. The men and women here have a long list of shit that has been going on. And for some time, it seems like." Henry asked him what he thought they were going to do now. "Grandda is here. He seems to think that this place will shut down soon. At least that's what he's saying to the men I've been talking to."

The fourth man was handing the board paperwork, his voice was deep with anger. Also, the loss of wages, which was what it was since Lily had taken it from them, was the least of their problems. Apparently, Lily had never put in for vacation for some of them, and they were still waiting to get paid for it—had been for the last several years.

"I'm sending you some help. Not that I think you're going to need it, but I'm sending you a financial attorney that has all the amounts owed to each of them in that hospital. As well as those that have left because of Lily." There was a long pause. Adrian waited while Henry spoke to someone in his office.

61

"Adrian, I want you to remain calm for a bit. Apparently, more things against Miss Lily have been turned up."

He asked what it was, but Henry was laughing too hard to tell him. When he told him he'd talk to him later, Henry just laughed more. Whatever was going down, it wasn't going to help keep this place open.

When the door behind them was banged against the wall, Adrian as well as the others stood up. Christ, he was really in a shitstorm here. Adrian thought it was just as funny as Henry had when he became a part of the meeting with him.

Chapter 5

Meghan called Ivy again. This was ridiculous. They'd been meeting for breakfast or lunch every day since they'd arrived, and now when she had something important to tell her, she wasn't around. Stomping her foot as she hung up the phone, Meghan went to the little place on her own. Meghan so hated to eat alone.

Carter, another Whitfield, was in there with an elderly gentleman. Meghan thought that he, too, was a Whitfield, but couldn't keep the large family straight. When she sat down at her usual table, Mr. Whitfield as well as Carter came to sit with her. Under the circumstances, she decided that she'd rather eat alone.

"Hello, dear. What do you have on your plate today?" Meghan told Mr. Whitfield that she was looking for Ivy. "I think her and Adam are furniture shopping today. Something about not having enough chairs for the dining room. You must be very happy for Ivy. Her and Adam make a great pair, don't you think?"

"Ivy? No, you must be mistaken. She won't date, much less

63

go furniture shopping with someone. She detests shopping as much as I love it. No, there isn't any way that she'd be doing such a thing." She looked at Carter when she laughed. "Do you know where she is?"

"Yes. She's shopping with Adam. As you were told." Meghan didn't like the way the woman was talking to her and decided that she wasn't hungry enough to sit with them. But as soon as she stood up, Carter told her to sit. "Now, we're not lying to you that she's with Adam. Nor about the fact that they're shopping. You do know that they're getting married, don't you?"

"Married? How on earth could you even think that? Ivy and I have only been here for a few days. A week. There isn't any way that she's met with someone and decided to marry them in that short time. Besides, Ivy doesn't even care to date, much less marry someone." Meghan looked at them both, wondering if what they were saying could be true. What would she do without her sister by her side? They were all they had, just the two of them. "I'm assuming that the guy you say she's marrying is another Whitfield. I mean, I might have met him at some point, but I can't see him wanting to marry my sister. She's brilliant, sweet, and kind. That's why I know that she'd tell me if she was thinking of getting married."

"I'm sure that you were going to be told. From what I understand, she's signing on to work with my grandson, Evan. They're forming a partnership even as we speak." Meghan knew then that they weren't lying to her. Ivy had spoken of nothing else but how much she was enjoying working for the other man. "I'm sorry, honey. But I'm betting that with her working with my boy and getting things squared away with her old boss, it slipped her mind."

"Thank you." Mr. Whitfield nodded. "We've been so close

for so long. We were all we had since we were children. I probably got too…. Well, I was very dependent on my sister — too much, I guess you could call it. And when I asked her to take me on this trip, it was for me to just blow off some steam. And to spend some alone time with her." Meghan thought of how whiney she sounded. "I'm sorry. I sound like a child that hasn't had a nap."

"Not at all. I can understand that on some level. It's difficult to have to share something that has only been yours for a long time. Like teddy bears or some shit like that." Meghan laughed and felt better for it. "I have to tell you, Meghan, I don't think that your sister is leaving here. She and Adam are mates. And I'm sure that you know what that is."

"She said something like that." Mr. Whitfield nodded when she looked at him. "We were going to the coast. I think she was going to give her notice too. I don't know why she's not been here for me too. Or even to tell me — Are you sure that she's here to stay?"

"Yes, she is staying. Or if she decides not to for some reason, Adam will go with her. It's the only way that he can be happy." Meghan just looked at the menu that was in front of her. If she'd been asked, she couldn't tell anyone if she'd ordered or not. She told Carter and Carter's grandda-in-law that she didn't know what to do now. "You don't have to worry about a thing. Not anything now that we're going to be related. I have a couple of houses that you can choose from. They're not as big as Adam's — he and Ivy really are out shopping. But you can live in one of them houses that I got for as long as you want." Mr. Whitfield took her hand into his rough callused ones.

"I never thought that she'd marry. Not after what had happened to her at home." Carter asked her what had happened. "This man, I don't think they ever caught him, started saying things about her that weren't true. I believe one of them was that she had carried his child and aborted it. This was all put in the paper, and they wouldn't tell anyone who had given them the information. The police told us that their hands were tied on this. That whoever wanted to could put whatever they wanted in the paper, true or not. His free speech got her into all kinds of trouble. I think that is another reason that she was so willing to go with me to the coast."

Carter started making notes as she bombarded her with question after question. How many lies had been printed? Was anyone else at the paper willing to talk to the police? And the one that seemed to have pissed Carter off the most, was the hospital added to the rumors by saying that they'd seen things as well.

When a platter of food was set in front of her, Meghan pushed it away. She wasn't sure that she could hold anything down right now. But Carter shoved it back at her and told her to eat. Meghan picked up her fork and took several bites before she realized that the woman was treating her like a child.

"No, I'm not. But you need to keep your strength up to deal with all this. Ivy will need you." Meghan looked at Mr. Whitfield, then back at Carter. Meghan was sure that she'd not voiced anything about being treated this way. "You didn't. I can read your mind. I don't think you have to worry about not being useful around here—none of us think badly of you. Your sadness of Ivy seemingly leaving you is unfounded. The other things that you've done? I'm not worried about that. But I would like to tell you that you are right that Ivy needed this more than you did. And I think that you're an amazing sister for making sure that she loosened up and had some fun. Even arguing with you, it's a stress reliever for you both."

Tears filled her eyes as she sat there. These people, they'd been nothing but kind to both her and Ivy since they had arrived. Meghan was sure that they were only doing it for her because of Ivy. But at this point in her life, she would take a friendship any way that she could get it.

"When we were informed about our parents getting a divorce, Ivy rushed home to be with me. She'd already gone away for college by then. When our parents filed for divorce, I think it was somewhat of a relief to both of us. All they did was argue, slam doors, and even going so far as to threaten each other with bodily harm." Ollie, as he'd asked her to call him, said that she and Ivy were lucky to have each other. "Yes. We are. However, at the time, all I could think about was that our parents were going to kill each other if they didn't do this right then. I don't know what I'd do if Ivy were to leave me. She's the best thing that has ever happened to me. And I love her with all my heart."

"You're a good girl, Meghan. And you're both very lucky to have each other." Ollie smiled at her, then nodded at her now empty plate. "You were a might hungrier than you thought, I'm thinking. How about you and me, we mosey on over to them houses of mine, and we'll see which of them suits you? Don't matter to me if you take one or not, or which one you have your eye on, you can stay there for the rest of your days for all I care."

The generosity of these people was amazing to her. They were there for someone whenever they needed it—they didn't even have to be related to them, opening their hearts and their home so that others could be safe and sound. Looking at Carter, Meghan wondered why she was so afraid of them—all of them, for that matter. Meghan figured that it had more to do with her and Ivy just having each other rather than them having a closed heart to others.

As soon as she paid her check, which never ceased to astonish her at how low it was, she and Ollie went to see the houses. Meghan had just eaten a breakfast of ham, bacon, and sausage, as well as two eggs and sausage gravy in a side bowl. And the fluffiest biscuits she'd ever eaten. There was a crock of butter on the table, honey, as well as an assortment of jams. Nothing could compare to that and looking at houses.

The first house that they looked at reminded her of Tara in that movie about Rhett and Scarlett. There were pillars out front on a porch that just looked like it was begging to be sat on. The rockers there, even though it was cold, looked inviting and nice. When they opened the door, it spilled into an entrance hallway that took her breath away. The entire house was just like the front hall, spectacular and welcoming.

The next two were just as beautiful and as large as the first one. There were three bedrooms on the second floor, and the master suite at the end of the long hallway. Ollie told her that he knew this group of men from the pack that would take an old house and bring it up to par. This one, he told her, had had five bedrooms, but they'd been small. Meghan fell in love with the kitchen of the second house.

"Well now, I won't rush you about this." She told him that she would love to rent the first one from him, just until she got herself something smaller. "I'm sorry, darling, I never meant for you to pay rent. The house is yours to live in if that's what you want. I have no use for so many homes, and I'd be glad if you were to take if off my hands. And I don't much care what you do to it either, so long as you don't burn it to the ground or paint it some ungodly color."

"No, I'd never do that. I love the wood siding on it. The backyard that just screams for someone to sit out and watch it. I love the pool as well. But, I can't live there rent free. That wouldn't be right." He told her that she was doing him a favor by living in it. "A favor for you? How exactly does that work?"

"Well, I don't have to worry about squatters or the such. Not that we have much trouble with that, but you just don't know about people nowadays. And if you're living there in the house, you're only a hop and a skip away from your sister's home. I should have pointed that out right away." Meghan was charmed. Not just because of the house, but also the elderly man too. He was so sweet that she couldn't help herself. She kissed him on the forehead. "Now, you're gonna make some man jealous if he were coming around. Kissing an old man like me — well, it surely does feel good. I thank you for it."

Laughing and crying at how wonderful she felt, her and Ollie made arrangements for her things to be brought from her rental back home. They also made plans for her to be able to go to the barn. It was a large building that sat at the back of his son's property, he told her. It had all kinds of things that they'd been saving.

"I don't know why we save so much. Hard to part with it — memories, I guess. Like my Adam. It took him getting a mate for him to finally fill the house with things that weren't as old or older than his daddy is." She laughed with him. "I'm so happy, Meghan. You did this old man a solid, you did."

Meghan still wasn't sure that the arrangement was working out to the best advantage for Ollie. But she'd have her own home, for a while anyway, and her things around her. Yes, Meghan thought, she might well like living here.

~*~

Ivy made her way around the hospital. It wasn't large, but it had so much charm that she couldn't help but be happy to be here. Evan had made sure that she was known to the people that worked there with him, as well as set her up with an office close to his.

"I don't go there much. But it's nice to have it when I have a patient in post-op. Saves me having to go home to nap and come back." She told him that she usually slept in an empty room when she had to stay. "Yes, but my wife? She gets a little testy when I'm not close to her."

Ivy didn't comment. She had noticed that all the mates to the Whitfield men were constantly touching and hugging their other halves. She thought about Adam and what they'd done last night.

She'd been in the kitchen, making herself a sandwich since she'd missed lunch, when he came up behind her, wrapping his arms around her waist. Ivy had leaned back into his chest and they'd stood that way until she turned toward him.

"I'm not sure what I'm supposed to do." He asked her what she wanted to do. "Sex. I want to have sex with you. But as I told you, I'm not that good at it."

"Perhaps it was your partner and not you." Ivy looked into his eyes to see if he was making fun of her. "Never. I'd never make fun of you when something so serious as sex is being discussed."

She still hadn't been sure what to do with him, so she kissed him though it was such a mundane word for what it was. And nothing in this world could have prepared her for the connection that seemed to want to take her to her knees.

Adam touched her everywhere, or so it felt like he had. And when he took her breast into his mouth, nibbling on the tip before taking it entirely into his mouth, she held on to him, keeping him there. Ivy never wanted him to stop what he was doing. Nor did she want him to leave her.

When he pulled back from her, she whimpered. The cool breeze that blew across her breast made her nipple tighten even more. Her body warmed to an almost molten feeling. And when he took a step back from her, giving her the feeling that he was rejecting her, Ivy felt her temper snap. She was sure now that it had been her own insecurities that had her doing that.

"I told you I wasn't good at this. The least you could have done was not to—" Her feet slipped out from under her when Adam pulled her to him for another devasting kiss. Ivy held onto him, fearful that she'd burst apart if he rejected her again.

"I want you with every beat of my heart. I will never turn you away, ever, when we come together. I pulled away because we're about to have company." The doorbell sounded then, the loveliest melody she'd ever heard for such a thing. "I can smell them, if you're wondering. One of them is your sister, the other my mom. I do not want to be caught necking in the kitchen with you. You have no idea how much I'd like to send them away and take you right here on this counter."

She'd been flustered when she made her way into the living room where his family was. Her sister looked so happy, Ivy was actually envious of whatever had made her that way. Knowing that they both had had some issues—her with her job and Meghan being upset with her about little things that they had no control over—Ivy wanted her to be just as happy as she was.

Taking a seat in the overstuffed chair that had been claimed by her as soon as she sat in it, she tried not to think about what had just happened. Or what hadn't happened because of the interruption. Eve had smiled at her, and Ivy thought that she knew somehow. That her and Adam had come so close to having sex that she was embarrassed by it.

"Are you paying attention?" She looked at the man that was sitting across her desk from her. She did not remember his name, or how he'd gotten into her office. "I was asking you if you were planning to hang around here."

"I'm still trying to figure that out." The man, when he smiled reminded her of the shark specials that she and Meghan watched every year. He seemed to be all teeth and no heart.

Ivy wasn't sure where that had come from. She never judged people based on a first impressions, but this man made her skin crawl. Ivy was suddenly afraid. While she didn't know where that feeling had come from, it shook her confidence level a great deal.

"That's good. I'd hate for this hospital to not have you around here." The little touch that seemed to be behind his eyes startled her when Sunny spoke to her.

I'm on my way to your office. If he asks, which I don't think he will, you and I are going out to do a little baby shopping, then going home. Ivy knew from experience that she only had to think of the other person and she could converse with them. However, she'd no idea why Sunny could do it. *I'm magical. Seriously, I'm going to have to show you the things I can – Never mind. I'm on my way now.*

When she stepped into the office, her hand on her large belly, the man with her disappeared. Ivy stood up, then sat back down. Lightheaded, she was glad that someone was there to help her. Sunny was holding her head down between her legs as she cursed. She was good at it too. Some of the words she used, Ivy was sure, hadn't been meant to string together.

"I'm all right now." When she lifted her head, Sunny took the seat that the man had been in. "Either you killed him with your *magical* shit or he was a vampire. Did you kill him?"

"What made you jump there, I wonder? I didn't, just so you know. But I was ready to do the deed. He's gone because he knew as soon as he smelled me that he was up the creek without a motor." Ivy told her with a laugh that she'd said it wrong. "No matter. He's gone, but I have a feeling that he'll be back."

"Why? Who is he, and what have I done to have him coming here to my office?" Sunny said that she didn't know but would get something from the chair. Ivy looked at the chair, then back at her. "I told you the other day, you would not believe the shit I can do now. I died, did you know that? This vampire guy, Tanner, brought me back, then helped guide me to the Whitfields. I think that he and his fae live in the lower levels of Carter's home. Though I'm not sure of that. He moves—"

"I think you're getting off subject here. I could be wrong, but I think we were talking about my visitor." Sunny smiled at her, and Ivy smiled as well. "I know that I'm going to hate myself for asking this, but what do you mean, smelled you?"

"I'm working on changing the subject so that you can calm down. Your heart rate was pretty high and I didn't want you to pass out." Ivy told her that she was much better now. "Good. The vampire that was here, he was sent. I'm working on figuring out who did it. It's a little harder to trace a young one, because they're colder blooded. That guy, he was only about two hundred years old."

"I do hope that you realize that two hundred years old is very old to me." Sunny smiled again. "Or was this a way to calm me again? I assure you, I'm just fine now."

"It's not. He is young at two hundred. However, and you'll have to meet him soon, Tanner is a good deal older. By like thousands of years older." Ivy wasn't sure how to process that, so she asked her if she'd gotten anything from the chair yet. "Not yet, no, but I'm going to ask Tanner to come here. He will know the scent, as well as some background on the other man. Then I can work with the rest."

"The rest how?" Sunny told her. "So, you have this, and I

quote here, 'freaky shit going on in your mind.' And that makes it so you can track a person and anyone that they've had contact with as well. I don't know if you're aware of this or not, but this isn't helping me. That guy was sent here for some reason, by someone you don't know, and you're going to find him with help from an old vampire."

"See, I knew that you'd get it." Ivy just shook her head. "Okay, the vampire, Tanner, is coming to meet you. And I'd advise you to give him just a taste of your blood. I know that you've shared with Adam, and you should with him as well. This way, if anything were to happen to you, myself or Tanner would be able to find you—"

"Hold on there a minute. I didn't let Adam have any of my blood." Her face got red when she thought of the kitchen again. "I think I'd remember that, don't you?"

"Did you have sex with him?" A personal question, but Ivy shook her head, sort of nervous about what Sunny would tell her. "You did something with him. I'm not saying that to embarrass you or anything, but we can all smell him on you. And he must have—I don't know, necked with you some, and he might have nipped your skin without you knowing it."

"And him doing that, it makes us bonded?" Sunny explained. "Oh. I didn't.... So, without having sex with him, I'd never be fully bonded to him. We'll be mated yes, but not fully bonded."

"That's right. I'm not telling you to run home and have sex with him—and you should know that the Whitfield men really know how to have sex—but it wouldn't hurt you. It might even let a little steam off from you both." Sunny smiled at her. "Like I said, you'll certainly get more out of it than you'd ever thought of."

"I don't feel good about this subject." Sunny stood up, her

smile plastered all over her face. "I don't think I like you overly much right now."

"Sure you do. I'm lovely and cuddly." She seemed to consider it, her hand on her chin and all. "Nah, not cuddly, but I am one person that you'd want to have at your side if shit ever hits the fan. The others would be any one of the Whitfields. The mates included."

"Is there a reason that I might need them or you by my side?" Sunny's smile fell from her face. It was as if someone had pulled a shade over her good humor. "If you know something, I'd like to know about it. I like to be prepared when it comes for me."

"Joshua has been doing some research on you and your sister. Not just your personal things, but people who might have had a grudge against the two of you." Ivy asked her what he'd found about them. "Not you two, not directly I guess, but your past, he told me, is about to come up and bite you in the ass if we're not there for you. I was headed to his office when I felt that you needed me."

"How can you feel that since we've never exchanged blood, nor have I touched you that I can remember?" Sunny told her that she didn't need to touch her because she had Adam. "I don't understand that. Oh, it's that tracking thing you can do. I'm assuming since you touched Adam, or perhaps Eve, or either of the Ollie men, then you have a tag of me."

"Yes, that's part of it." Sunny looked out the door before talking again. "You have other people to meet, other beings that will help you. You're going to need it. And not just for you, but for your sister too."

"How do you know?" Sunny shrugged. "Are you not telling me because you don't know? Or are you afraid of me freaking out? I can assure you, I'm made of stronger stuff than that."

"Yes, you are. But your sister is not." When she left her, Ivy started to think. Her sister, she was in trouble. From whom? She had no idea. But she'd fucking find out, and Ivy would protect her with her life.

No longer in the mood to think about what she wanted to do in her office in the way of décor or even just curtains or shades, Ivy left the hospital and decided to go and find Adam. He'd told her last night that he couldn't lie to her. She was going to test that now.

Chapter 6

Adrian answered all the questions put to him as he waited his turn to go to the podium. Yesterday had been a nightmare. Not for him, but for the people that had come into the meeting with him and the four board members. In addition to Henry, the Feds had come in to help with clean up and fall out, as well as a couple of other people from the White House.

It was said to anyone who asked that they were there on behalf of the president. Adrian didn't inquire but let the events of the last twenty-four hours roll around in his head. And now, here he was again, in front of a lot of people, and he was going to inform them of what they'd found from his investigation. Dylan and Grandda were standing with him.

"There sure are a lot of people out there. Why, they're lined up about butt hole to belly button." Adrian asked his grandda, not for the first time, if there was a book of his quotes where someone could read them. "I don't know, son. I just call it like I sees it. You have to admit, it's about as true as it can be."

"Yes, it is. However, if you could refrain from projecting the hillbilly for a while, I'll be forever grateful to you." He just laughed, and Adrian shook his head. "I don't know why this is being made to be such a big deal. I mean, they've arrested Lily and charged her with a lot of things I didn't even know about. And the hospital is getting a major overhaul when it comes to not just the board but finding more doctors and nurses."

"They have to have this out in the open. Let the people know that they're not going not put up with this shit anymore." Adrian just looked at Carter. "What? You don't believe me?"

"No, I believe you. But still, this didn't need this much fanfare, I don't think." His name was called, and he went up to the podium, and waited while it seemed like fifty lights from cameras went off in front of him. "Good afternoon. My name is Adrian Whitfield, acting governor for the state of Ohio. I'm here to ask—"

"What do you have to say about the parents of one of your sisters-in-law?" "Have you found out anymore about the missing men?" "I'd like for you to tell me when the rest of the state is going to see you."

Adrian didn't bother answering the questions that were thrown to him. They had nothing to do with what he was there for, so Dylan told him to ignore them. What he said up here now, it was going to set the tone for the rest of his elections. And he didn't want that haunting him.

"Mercy Hospital has been closed down for an upgrade for the next month or so. My sister-in-law was working there when she met my brother. Because of her explanations of things that she'd encountered, I and some of my family did a detailed investigation into some other allegations that have been put before the board there. What we found was far more than we had expected." He looked down at the list of things that had been found and the marks next to the ones that he could share. The police department, as well as some people from the White

House, had gone over everything. "Yesterday, late yesterday afternoon, I came here on behalf of Doctor Ivy Walton Whitfield, surgeon. She was being harassed by Lily Donaldson, the head of the hospital and boss of Doctor Whitfield. In the investigation of her ill treatment of her, it was discovered that not only had she been skimming money from the hospital, she was also taking advantage of her position here."

A woman stood up; she had neither paper nor microphone as most of the others did. She told them her name, Victoria James, ER doctor. After clearing her throat several times, she began to talk.

"I worked at Mercy, like a great many other people that are here today. Most of the others were fired or were forced to quit when Donaldson decided that we could no longer have vacation time. Also, we were forbidden to treat a certain clientele. Additionally, we had to make sure that they had insurance as well as money before treating them." She looked around the room, then back up at him. "I lost my husband because of her. He wouldn't be there for me when I could no longer be there even for myself. I was working, as many of us were required to do, eighty to a hundred hours per week. Most of the time triple shifts, because so many of the others left. Ivy, she was one of the best surgeons that I've had the pleasure of working with and stood up for the nurses several times—until such time that they had to ask her to stop, as it was harder for them, you see. Donaldson would make it horrendous for them. I would like to thank you. Thank you from the bottom of my heart for your making a difference around here. You will have my vote at whatever you do, Mr. Whitfield."

Adrian hadn't expected that. He admired the woman for realizing why he'd done this. Adrian asked her to please find one of his staff when this was over to see if the accounting that they had on Donaldson was accurate about unpaid time.

He turned questions that he didn't know the answer to over to the men from the different agencies that were helping look into this. Adrian did answer a lot of them, mostly about how the things had been found, and after that, how he had reported it to the proper people so that justice could be found.

Another hour went by, and he was beginning to feel like, for some reason, he'd failed these people. Adrian knew that he'd not been in charge of such things, and had it not been for Ivy, he wouldn't have known either, but someone should have. And he wanted to find out why they hadn't.

People started whispering when he was coming off the stage. He would have thought he'd not be able to hear people whispering, but with so many in the room, butt hole to belly button as Grandda had said, the whole of it would be loud. He was called back to the podium when he recognized Henry standing there waiting for him.

"Ladies and gentlemen, if you were to give me a moment or two of your time now, I'd very much appreciate it." Everyone seemed to be blown away by the president coming to their town. "I cannot stay long—I have a few things going on right now." The twitter of laughter had Adrian relaxing a little. "When I heard what was going on here in this fine town, I knew that I had to have a closer look at things. Adrian's name, as you can well imagine, has been coming to me for the last month or so. But with this, I felt that it was something that I'd have to thank him for myself. He's done you all very proud with this. No town should ever be without a medical unit nearby."

Adrian shook his hand, then was pulled in for one of those manly hugs. He hadn't expected Henry to be there, nor did he think that anyone else had. After Henry shook the hand of his grandda and Carter, he waved to the crowd of people and left the building. Adrian just stood there feeling like he'd been hit between the eyes. Then the questions began anew.

They asked how long he'd known the president. Did he endorse him going to the senate? A few people even asked if he was going to run for president when the time came. He smiled at the crowd and knew that this was what Henry had planned when he'd come here today. Henry wanted him to throw his hat into the race for presidency soon.

"Yes, I do plan to run for senate. And President Cobb has been a good friend of the family for some time. He has encouraged me to run not just for the governor seat that came up, but also for other things that would get me to the White House." The questions then were too many, and with all of them being shouted toward him, Adrian didn't know how to answer them. Grandda joined him at the podium then, and simply put his hand up and the room quieted.

"Most of you know me. And my family." A lot of people shouted that they were good people. "Thank you. Me and my family, we sure do thank you for making Adrian here feel so welcome. And we're thankful that he's working so hard to make this state a place where others might like to live."

After a little more of Grandda talking him up, he led him off the stage and into the awaiting car. They were expected home, the three of them. Adrian leaned back in his seat as soon as Carter joined them.

"You did good up there, Adrian." He asked Carter if she'd known that Henry had been going to join them. "Sure, I did. And the reason I didn't tell you is, I wanted you to look just as surprised as the rest of them were. It plays better on the television that way."

Adrian would have gladly strangled her if he wasn't so afraid she'd hurt him. When she laughed, he knew that she was invading his mind and let her see how he was going to hurt her. Not that he would. He loved this woman as much as he did his brothers. She was just a pain in his ass.

"All right. Lily Donaldson is in jail. She has a trial date set for some time after the new year. I'm thinking that they want to gather up as much as they can, simply to make a better case. That's what I'd do." He asked her what she thought was going to happen to her. "Don't know for sure, but a lot of people want her hung out to dry. Most of the board too. By the way, not only are your parents staying on the board, they've been asked to find trustworthy men and women to be there too."

"So, this is done?" Carter told him that she thought it was only the start. "What do you mean? You think they'll find more shit out about this place?"

"Could be, but I doubt it. But what I meant was, there will be a good many other hospitals that will be taking better care with their staff. No one wants the president and future president coming in and taking over." Adrian could imagine that. He laid his head back and closed his eyes. "Adrian, you need to be aware that you're going to have to start beefing up your security. I know that you can take care of yourself, but you'd be better off having men around you that you can trust. And soon."

"You can be in charge of it. You and the rest of the Whitfield women. Not my mom though. She'll have me wearing protective gear all the time. And my mate, if she comes around, won't be able to find me." They were all laughing when he got out of the car at his home.

Adrian wanted to just go in, get into his bed, and forget the day. But he'd promised Adam that he'd help him get the soil ready for the peas that they planted each year in late winter. His mom could make the best creamed peas that were ever made, as far as he was concerned.

He waited for his brother to come by for an hour. Adrian didn't want to call him out, tell him about schedules, so he didn't. Adam wouldn't miss working with him unless it was an emergency. With a new mate, he'd bet his last dollar that she was the reason that he wasn't showing up. And Adrian didn't even care. He was too exhausted to do much of anything right now.

Going into the house, stripping down as he made his way up the stairs, Adrian thought for sure that he could very easily sleep for a month. Not even bothering with putting on his lounge pants, he fell into the bed. Whatever happened for the rest of the day, he was officially done.

Closing his eyes, he didn't even feel sleep come over him. It was like he'd been hit by a freight train and it had knocked him out. His last thought was, if only being governor affected him like this, he could only imagine what being president would bring to him.

~*~

Adam was losing ground every day, it seemed lately. Just yesterday he'd meant to put in an order and had completely forgotten it. The seeds that he was going to plant for fun weren't a big deal to not have for one more day, but he hated to not have his ducks in a row. Bending over his paperwork again, he looked up when he heard someone. Ivy was standing there, leaning against the door.

"Are you busy?" He started to tell her how frustrated he was with himself when she continued. "Yesterday I had a little talk with your family. They are blunt and right to the point, aren't they? Anyway, I was going to talk to you about it last night, but I was on call and had to leave you."

"What sort of bluntness was it?" Instead of answering him,

she took a step toward him, pulling her blouse up and over her head. Then she dropped it to the floor. "I see. I'm assuming it was one of my brothers' mates that you spoke with."

"Yes. I guess that everyone knows what you did with me in the kitchen. I didn't know." By now she was kicking her shoes off, along with her pants. "I'm thinking that we should get some things straight, don't you?"

"Yes. No. I have no idea. The moment that you took your blouse off, I couldn't hear any more." Ivy asked him if he needed a doctor. "Yes. I mean, if you're meaning like I think you are, then yes, I very much need medical help."

Adam stood up when she stood in the middle of the room. He wanted to rush her, to knock her to the floor and take her. But this was a game, a tease for them both, and Adam was thrilled to death to be playing with her. He took his belt off. Then he ripped off the T-shirt that he'd been wearing.

"You've put me through the ringer. I've wanted to take you, in any way that you'd allow me to, since I met you." Her body warmed at his words—he could smell every part of her body lusting for his. Instead of going to her, doing anything to her, he needed to know why she was doing this. "I've been thinking of making love to you for several days. The thought of having you naked beneath me, having you scream out my name—"

"No, that's not what I want." His heart seemed to come to a screeching halt. Even his breath had soured in his lungs, his disappointment was so keen. "There isn't any reason that you can't be beneath me, is there? Unless you want to do this your—"

"No! I mean, no. I don't want to do it my way. I'll do whatever you wish." She nodded and came closer to him. "You have no idea how much I've needed you. I wanted to give you time to trust me but taking cold showers several times a day was getting hard to explain. Especially since I'm not —"

"Adam, shut up." His teeth came together so hard that he felt like his teeth had nearly shattered. "Strip for me. Then I want you to sit at your desk. In your chair. I've never done this before, so if it's wrong, you'll let me know, right?"

"Nothing you could do to me from this moment on could ever be wrong."

He stepped back around his desk. When he seated himself, Adam had to stand again to adjust his cock twice. He'd never been so hard nor so aroused in his life. Adam remembered that she'd told him to strip, and he peeled his pants off, as well as his shoes and socks, in one motion. Looking up when she said his name, Adam swallowed twice, then two more times before he trusted himself to speak and not beg. Ivy was naked. And his.

"You are the most beautiful thing I've ever seen. If I were to go blind at this moment, the memory of you standing before me like this would be all that I needed to sustain me for the rest of my days." She flushed, her cheeks pinking up so much that her freckles disappeared. "I love you, Ivy Walton Whitfield. Take me."

She sat on his desk and he wanted to take her then, shove everything off, uncaring of whatever broke, just to taste her. Instead he smoothed his hands over her skin. The warmth of her calves, her toes, even her knees made him harder still. At this rate he'd be dead, with only a smile on his face for others to wonder about.

It took her several moments to get where she seemed to be most comfortable. Adam had been told no less than a dozen times to keep his hands to himself. It was dizzying to watch her and not be able to touch her. When she leaned back on his desk, mindful of his paperwork, he looked her in the eyes as he slid his hand down her inner thigh.

Sliding his finger into her heat had her screaming out his name, coming so hard that Adam could feel her tightening around his finger. Leaning over her, inhaling her scent that would be his for a lifetime, Adam licked her from gate to nubbin. She gave him the richness of her body and he was able to taste her nectar while it flooded his mouth. Adam needed her, but first, he wanted her peaking several times more times yet. Then she screamed for him.

He couldn't wait. Couldn't be satisfied with just tasting her. Adam stood up and lifted her by her lovely ass, and Ivy wrapped her legs around him as he took her to the wall. Falling to the floor, he rolled to take most of it. Adam looked up at her as she sat up, her legs around his hips.

"I want to ride you." Adam nodded. "Help me, Adam. I'm in agony just thinking about how you're going to fill me. Bring me again and again. Then I want to bite you, draw your blood into mine."

Helping her to rise up over him, Adam was nearly cross-eyed when she started to slide down his cock. Every time she had a tiny, heart stopping climax, he would too. There was more to come and he could not wait to have her—

"Holy Christ, that's it." He held her hips while she rode him. Adam couldn't breathe well, couldn't think beyond what she was doing to him. And when she leaned down, her breast touching his chest, he held her there and took her mouth.

He kissed her savagely, leaving her no doubt that he hungered for her, needed her so badly. And when she offered her neck to him, her hand pulling on his nipple, Adam bit down just as she sank her teeth into his shoulder. Christ, he thought, she had actually killed him.

Adam cried out, his climax surpassing any he'd had before.

Even the feeling of her coming around him had him holding her slim body to his. Rolling her to her back, he took her much harder than he had thought he would, pounding her with his body brutally. And when his body came again, with him thinking that saying he was coming with his mate seemed so mundane for how he felt, Adam bit her again, this time so deeply that he heard bones breaking, felt her blood fill him to the point of being giddy with her offering.

"Again, Adam. Please, I beg of you, make me come again."

He didn't think he had it in him. As it stood now, he wasn't sure that he could even walk. But not wanting to disappoint his Ivy, Adam took her breast into his mouth even as he made love to her slowly this time. He wanted to satisfy her, make her know that he wasn't a brute, but someone that loved her dearly, worshipped her like none other. And when he kissed her once more, taking his time with reaching the darkest, richest part of her mouth, she moaned. Adam even enjoyed the taste of that small thing, knowing that he was the happiest man alive.

Ivy came three times as he made love to her. She was so responsive, so loving. And when he felt his own release racing over him, he kissed her again, felt her nails dig deeply into his flesh.

Realizing that he'd passed out, whether from exhaustion or just simply the best sex that he'd ever had, Adam woke to find that at some point, he'd rolled to his back, and Ivy was atop him with a lap blanket from the sofa pulled over the two of them. Holding her, hearing her heart beating, her breaths blowing gently over his naked flesh, Adam closed his eyes and held her. When his brother nudged at his mind, Adam told Blake to go away, to leave him to his peace.

I'd like to, big brother, but I have something I need your help on. It's concerning something I found out about the woman that came to your house blaming you for the boy, Nathan. His name is Nathan Hitchcock. Parents are Welham and Evelyn Hitchcock. The kidnapper is Shelby Crock. He asked him if it could wait. *I would like to tell you that it could, but I'm afraid that it can't. She's out now — on bail, apparently — and no one knows how that came to happen. Also, about the little boy; his parents have taken him to the hospital and left him there. I haven't figured out why they did such a thing, or where they are now. The house is being packed up. The drivers of the rigs have very little information other than that they were told to pack up the house and to donate it all to the local charities. One of them even asked me if they could take what they wanted of it first. I had no idea what to tell him, so I thought I'd contact you.*

Okay, good to know. But what does that have to do with me? I mean, I don't have any idea where they've gone either. Blake said that he knew that. *I have a feeling that you're trying very hard to give me time to absorb something. Tell me, Blake.*

Nathan tried to kill himself last night. He was staying with his parents, of course, but when they dropped him off at the hospital, I guess they told him that he wasn't wanted. He asked him how he'd done it. *Sheets tied together so that he could hang himself in the bathroom. If it hadn't been for the nurses coming on duty, he might well have died. They were doing a bed check for the next shift and had started with his room, rather than end with it. I guess they have a routine they follow, and they broke it and ended up in his room just in time.*

Adam didn't want to do it, but he woke Ivy. After telling her what had happened, she got up and started pulling on her clothing. He put on what was left of his — his shirt was torn to shreds, and he could only find one of his socks.

"Has anyone talked to him about what he did?" Adam said that he didn't know and asked Blake. No, he said. No one had been in to see him, as he was still in intensive care. "I'm going to call Meghan. One of her many job choices was being a social worker. She was really good at it but frustrated by the red tape that came with the job. And I have a minor in psychopathology that I think might be able to help him as well."

"If you think that she can help him, I'll have one of my brothers pick her up and she can meet us at the hospital." Ivy told him that she thought that her sister was the best. "Good. I'll have Blake call her and then pick her up."

He remembered that he was to have met his brother at the farm to get the furrows ready for winter seeding things. Embarrassed by having to tell him that he was sorry, Adam was also happy as hell that Ivy had come to be his mate in all ways today.

By the time they got to the hospital, not only had Blake spoken to Meghan, he'd also beaten them there. They were waiting by the desk when he and Ivy made their way to the children's care unit on the third floor. The plan was to move him to the fourth, where they were better equipped to handle this sort of thing. Ivy didn't want that to happen. She worried a great deal about his safety.

Being a doctor of good standing and one of the family members that had brought order to the place, she was given permission to take her sister with her as she went to examine the young boy. Adam and Blake sat in one of the many chairs in the waiting room. Adam had a feeling this was going to take a while and leaned his head back against the wall. Blake did the same, not wanting to abandon him or Nathan.

Chapter 7

Ivy knocked on the door. No one answered her, so she moved into the room with her sister. The little boy on the bed wasn't moving, not even to look to see who had entered the room with him. She could almost taste the pain on Nathan. And that wasn't even taking into account his injuries from his thankfully failed attempt to take his own life.

"Hello. My name is Ivy Whitfield." That had him looking at her, more than likely remembering the name of his rescuer. "This is my sister, Meghan. We've just heard that your parents left you here. I'm sorry for that. Is there anything that I can do for you? I'd like to say that I think that they're bastards for doing it." He didn't react, not even to blink as he looked at her. Her heart broke for the little man.

"They said that I was no longer their kid. That they weren't going to take me back because that would stop the donations." Ivy felt her anger and hatred toward the unknown parents all the way to the bottom of her feet. "I don't have nobody now. That other woman was mean to me, but she didn't throw me away."

91

"You do have a lot of people, Nathan. There are a lot of people that are here for you and want to help you. Me especially." Ivy moved back and let Meghan continue. "I'm so sorry that they were mean to you like that. I would never do that to anyone—not to my son, or even just my friend. I know that I'd be just as hurt as you are had that happened to me. I don't have a great many friends here. I love this place, but I don't have any friends. I could use one like you. You see, my parents were horrible people too. They ignored us until they needed something. Treated my sister and I like we were bothering them all the time. Isn't that so sad? But I have to tell you, Nathan, something that's also the sweetest thing in the world. My sister and I, we love each other so much that I could never be without her."

"You got to be loved by someone though. Nobody wants me." Meghan said that she wouldn't mind having him with her. "You say that now, but what if the papers stop talking about you? You gonna shove me away too?"

"Heavens no." She smiled at him when he finally looked at her. "I would love to have you come and stay with me. I think we'd be good for each other. I've a lovely home, plenty of room for you and I to be in. Mr. Whitfield, he told me that I could live there forever if I wanted. And he'd be glad for it. To be honest with you, Nathan, I should have gone with the smaller home. This one is meant for a family, not just a woman that is starting over with things. A family like you and I could be."

Hope. It was there in his eyes for a spilt second, then gone again. But instead of not looking at them again, at least not directly, he would sneak peeks at them. Ivy sat down beside the bed and picked up his arm. There were marks there, marks that she was all too familiar with in her line of work. Someone had tied him up and left him.

Ivy knew that he'd been undernourished when he'd been brought here the first time. He was also dehydrated, as well as banged up a bit according to the file. Turning his hand over into her much larger one, Ivy asked him a few questions.

"Were you tied up? I mean, before she took you to Adam's house? When you lived with that nasty woman, did she hurt you more than just starving and hitting you?" Ivy didn't think he was going to answer her, but he finally nodded. "Did she make you stay outside a lot, too?"

"Yes, ma'am. Sometimes I think she forgot about me, and I'd be out there for days and days." Ivy knew that as a child, it would seem longer than it had been. But for some reason, she thought that he was dead on about how long he'd been there. "I never got to eat at the table either. I had to eat on the floor or outside." Ivy had to let go of his hand or accidently take her anger out on him. Putting her hands in her lap, she had to calm herself before she could speak again.

"Nathan, if they were here right now, I'd tie them up and make them eat on the ground every day. Not even giving them a plate to eat off of either." He grinned at her. "You know what else I'd do? I'd make sure that they paid for how they treated you. Going to jail for this? Well, it seems so little for what you've suffered."

Nathan glanced at Meghan, then back at her. When he spoke again, his voice was low, fear lacing an otherwise wonderful kid's voice. "Shelby used to make me pretend to run away so that she could come and find me. I was to go to houses that she looked at, and I was to let her in the house so she could take things." Ivy asked him if he knew where the things were that she'd gotten. "No, ma'am. I know she took some of it to a friend of hers. He wasn't nice to me either."

Ivy told Dylan and Carter what she'd found out through

their newly established links. The woman seemed to be mounting up charges right and left. Sunny asked her to ask Nathan if he knew where they'd lived. All they could find out about her address was that she had a post office box. She had a feeling that there was more to this than a little boy and stealing.

After she asked Nathan the questions, and he gave them the answers that the women needed, Nathan reached for Meghan's hand too. When he closed his eyes, falling asleep quickly, she looked over at her sister when she started to sob quietly.

"He's been dealt such a shitty hand, Ivy. I want to bundle him up and take him home with me right now." Ivy told her if she was serious, she and the Whitfields could make that happen. Ivy hoped that they'd help her, anyway. "Yes. The first time I saw him, I just simply fell in love with him. I don't know why I think this, but I believe we could be good for each other."

Reaching for Adam, she told him what was going on, the information that Nathan had given her, and how his sisters were looking into it. He told her that he was there for her should she need him, and that Blake had said that he was as well. This was what she loved about this family — they were a united front when necessary, but also knew when to leave someone alone.

Ivy examined Nathan as best she could without waking him. When his dinner tray came in, all the silverware plastic and nothing on it to harm him, the nurse who brought it in said that she was to watch over him the entire time. Ivy told her who she was and that she'd not allow him to harm himself. Not ever again.

"I hope not. Those people that brought him into this world, they need to be handed their asses if you don't mind me saying so. They're just not deserving of this little boy." Ivy agreed with her and told her that they were doing something about them as well. "I was down there when they brought him in, Doctor

Whitfield. You'd not believe what they said about him. And right there in front of his face. Telling us that he just wasn't the same. They'd not been able to see him grow up, and they didn't know if they could be a part of his life. I wanted to strangle them right then and there. Some people should not be allowed to breed if you ask me."

"I understand what you're saying. Being a surgeon and putting a few children back together when their parents did something horrific to them gave me nightmares." Nathan woke, and Meghan moved to help him set up his meal while Ivy took the nurse aside. "Could you make sure that Meghan is allowed to stay here with him? I think he'll do much better now that she's hoping to be a part of his life."

"I heard that she was going to adopt him. Adam and his brothers are on the phone right now getting her registered as a foster parent. Nice group of people, you Whitfields. I've never seen a one of you being hurtful or mean. I think it'll do them both some good, don't you?" She told her that she did. "All right. If you need me just pull the nurse's cord there. And I'll see what I can do about getting your sister another bed in here, or at least a comfy chair. Thank you."

"No, I thank you. Nurses like the ones here at this hospital are about the best that I've had the pleasure of working with and beside." Rachel, the nurse, told her that she appreciated that and would pass it along to the other nurses. "I'd like that. Again, thank you."

"I'll be bringing in Meghan another meal too. There isn't any sense in making her starve when she's doing such a good deed for us."

Ivy thanked her again and pulled Nathan's chart into the room with them. Writing orders for him to have Meghan there would save the butt of any of the nurses when questioned. Ivy put the chart away just as Meghan's tray was being delivered.

Finding Adam in the hallway near the closed off section that handled people and children like Nathan, she went to him willingly and wrapped her arms around him. In that moment Ivy knew that she loved him and would for the rest of her days. Looking up at him, she could see his love for her as it seemed to reflect back to her.

"I love you, Adam. I don't know what I would have done had you not been there for me. I think well before we even met that you had a place in your heart saved for me, and I did for you as well." He kissed her, gently and lovingly. "I want to have children with you. Lots and lots of them. I don't care if they're ours or someone else's that didn't deserve them in the first place. All right?"

"Yes. Blake, he's taking in children too, did you know that?" She shook her head. "Yes. Right now, he has it in the works to get two boys, both of them from a broken home. Neither of them have any trust for anyone, not even Blake. When he rescued them, he said that he wanted to find their parents and kill them."

"Are you telling me that we're going to have to be able to have an alibi when we take some in? I'm game if you are, but if push comes to shove, buck-o, you're on your own if it comes between you and the kids." He was laughing as they made their way to the elevator. "Oh, before I forget, we're hosting Thanksgiving this year. Your mom is kind of pushy about that sort of thing, isn't she?"

"You have no idea. But it'll be fun. And it's not like we don't have enough people to help prepare. I think that Nate will enjoy it as well. He's been complaining about feeding just the two of us when he'd like to feed the entire family." They held hands all the way to the car.

Not that she thought she'd leave, but Meghan promised to call if she wanted a break. As soon as they were home, Ivy opted for bed and Adam said he'd join her.

Once she showered, washing off the germs and other smells from her body that she'd picked up at the hospital, Ivy crawled into bed with a sleeping Adam. He wrapped her into his arms as soon as she laid down and kissed her on the back of the neck. For some reason that made her more relaxed than the shower had. It wasn't long before she was asleep.

~*~

Ollie loved his new job. It gave him a sense of pride, helping out at the restaurant, and he got to talk to people all day long. Now, today he was going to learn how to set up the coffee pot and brew the dark liquid that a lot of people seemed to crave. While Ollie had never acquired a taste for it, there were a lot of people that swore it was the nectar of the gods.

It was cold this morning as he walked to work. He didn't drive anymore. Ollie could see just fine, but he couldn't move the way he had when he was younger. His reaction time was much slower than he was comfortable with, so he walked when he could, or asked for a ride when he wasn't up to it.

"Good morning, Ollie. Are you ready for the day?" He grinned at Mildred and said that he was. "I'm glad to hear that. Oh, there is a man here to see you. I think he's in the bathroom. I'm not sure. Can you have a word or two with him before we open? I don't think this man is as kind as other vampires that I've known."

Ollie didn't know but a couple of vamps. One of them was living right here in town, having a house upgraded for himself. Tanner was about the best friend he'd ever had. And Ollie was so happy that he'd decided to hang around.

Ollie started reading the instructions for making a pot of

coffee as the man came to sit on the barstool in front of him. It wasn't anyone that he knew. The smile on his face didn't hide the fact that he had some very long and sharp fangs. Ollie let his cat take a little of him, something that he rarely did, to show the man that his teeth were by far much more dangerous than his were.

"Say what you gotta say and move on. I don't have time to mess with you, and even if I did, I'd not waste any of it hanging around with you."

The man looked around then back at him.

Ollie wasn't falling for that little trick, the man making him think there were others with him. Instead, he repeated himself—another thing that he did not like doing. Repeating himself got tiresome, and he wasn't into that today.

"I've been sent to talk to you. Or rather, have a conversation with you regarding the whereabouts of Tanner. You are acquainted with him, I'm to understand." Ollie didn't so much as blink at the man. "You will tell me where he is, or I'll make your life very difficult if you don't cooperate."

"Compulsion doesn't work on me. It might have at one time, but I'm immune to such things. Now, you tell me what it is you want with this Tanner feller and if I have any idea who or where he is, I might tell you. But I'd not count on it if'n I was you. I don't take kindly to being forced into anything at my age." The man looked around again, and this time Ollie could see just a little fear in his way of doing it. "I said, tell me what you want."

He felt it—the age-old feeling of youth, having a little more gumption that he'd had in the last twenty or so years. When Ollie stood up the man started to as well. But with a point to the chair from Ollie, the vamp sat down and put his head low on the table.

"He has a great deal of magic. It is said that he is more than likely the first of our kind. His power would be more than any vampire of my age to have and he'd know what to do with it all." Ollie asked him his name. "Sheppard."

The room suddenly tightened—Ollie had to sit, or he'd pass out. As it was now, he was having a hard time holding onto his cat, trying his best to understand what was happening. When he saw Tanner, he looked as if he was bigger than he remembered him being. His body was wider, and muscles were twitching around his flesh. Ollie could also see his fangs, sharp, like weapons that anyone would know meant their downfall. Even he felt fear of the man a man that had been his friend for more years than he could remember.

Sheppard was lifted from the chair, even going so far as to be plastered against the ceiling above them. Tanner neither moved nor spoke as Sheppard was sobbing for forgiveness, begging for his life. Ollie stayed where he was as five more men, all vampires, appeared there. He held his breath, he supposed so that they'd not see or even remember that he was in the room.

"You dare come here. You dare to even say my name while you are in my realm." Sheppard begged once again for his life. "I'm going to kill you, have no doubt. You're a worthless piece of dung, and you'll pay for the wasted time I use in dealing with such a creature as you. The council of vampires, they have been searching for you for a great many years. And I've been given full authority to destroy you."

Ollie would have gladly told them whatever they wished to know. He might have been just as happy as a pup getting his ears rubbed if they'd forget he was around. Even going so far as to tell them that he was a woman in the last days of breeding if they wouldn't harm him. He'd tell them in a way that not only would they believe it, but he would as well. Might even be willing to go into labor to prove it.

But they didn't even look in his direction, didn't make a single noise as Tanner dangled Sheppard over his head. Ollie glanced at his friend, and in that moment, he was terrified of the gentleman. Even though he'd done nothing to him, ever, Ollie could see his blood-filled eyes. The way that his fangs were just over his lower lip. His nails were as long as the fingers that they were hanging from. So, when Tanner turned to him, Ollie had a feeling that he wasn't so much seeing him, but that he only just realized that he'd forgotten him.

"Ollie. You are all right?" Ollie nodded and told him that he thought so. "Yes, I'm afraid that I've taken my anger out on this man and have frightened you. I meant you no harm, Ollie. You are now and will forever be my friend."

"I know that. I surely do. I might have soiled myself hadn't you of been." Ollie felt his face heat up in embarrassment. Not for what he'd said, but that he'd said anything at all. "You're a good man, Tanner. What did this here man want with you? If'n you don't mind me asking."

"He is the child of the man that I have been looking for. Randal. You remember him, do you not? And I have one of his children as well. She has given me a great deal of information, and I only need to know where he is staying. Wanda, she only managed to escape Randal's rule by a small margin. This man, he is another of his children, but he is as stupid as Randal if he thinks to catch me unawares."

Ollie had heard of this man Randal. He had met Randal once long ago, when Ollie was nothing more than a small cat finding his way in the world. Randal had captured him while he was out wandering around on the very land they lived on now. Another man, not a vampire, had saved him then, but had been killed in the process instead of Ollie. The last he'd heard, the council had been looking for Randal, as well as the kiss that he'd managed to force into coming to him in the name of power. Which, Ollie remembered, hadn't been that much then. He doubted that he'd had any more given to him — not the way that he acted today, anyway.

The man, Sheppard, was destroyed. It wasn't a slow death, as Ollie was sure that was what Tanner wanted. But watching his dust rain down around the room, Ollie knew that the next time Randal sent someone, it might well be Randal himself. Tanner sat down at the table Ollie had been sitting at and watched him try to get the coffee machine running.

"Here, my friend, I shall show you." The two of them worked on making the machine do what he needed it to do. Tanner, knowing him as well as he did, showed Ollie the way that he'd learned a great many things. But from Tanner showing him step by step. Ollie learned just how to put the glass pots on and how to change out the huge coffee filters and fill them again, and by the time the doors were opened, Ollie had five pots of the vile brew going and was sitting with Tanner again. "I shall have to kill him. You know that, do you not?"

"I do. He's been pestering you for some time now. While I trust your judgment in this, what will the council say about you doing so?" He told him that he had permission to kill Randal and to take his kiss. "How many are they? And I'm betting this upsets you so much, on account'a you think that you're going to have to kill them as well."

"Yes. From what I have learned from Wanda, most of the ones in the kiss were changed without permission. Nor did a very large portion of them take well to it. Many have died due to the man's evilness, going into the sun rather than face their time forever being a vampire. There are a great many of them that were meant to be something productive. Had families that could no longer be a part of their everyday lives. And many of those left behind, they starved or were killed by Randal when he didn't get his way. He is a horrific man and should have been put down many years ago." Ollie shivered. It was terrible to be treated like a plaything for such a monster. "All that to say, there are fewer than a dozen of them left from the hundreds that answered to him when he was a better person."

"I'm surely sorry about that. Gotta ask you though—how did you know that Sheppard was here?"

Tanner smiled and told him that he'd felt his anger. "And to have you that pissed off, as Dylan is so fond of saying, I knew that it had to be something terrible. I'm only glad that I was able to leave my home and come here. You have saved me a great deal of time and effort." Ollie asked him if he'd read Sheppard's mind. "I raped it so that, if he had lived through this, he wouldn't have been the man that he started out to be. I believe you call them a vegetable. He would have been much worse."

Ollie nodded. and as soon as the doors were unlocked, Tanner said that he had to go. Ollie asked him, just before he left, if he was safe. With a quick hug, the older man said that he would be now, but that he must be careful from now on— Randal was not one to give up so easily. Ollie told him that he would be.

The breakfast crowd was heavy this morning. It was almost lunch time before he had a spell where he could sit and enjoy his own meal. Looking around at the townspeople, Ollie wondered for a brief moment why he'd ever thought of leaving this place.

He surely did miss his wife and mate. She'd been his rock, his teacher, as well as the one person in the world that he could talk to like none other. Of course, Ollie made it to the cemetery that was at the back of their land, but it was getting a might cold for that, and he wasn't able to go as often. He knew he could ask someone and they'd do it without saying a word, but Ollie didn't want to be a burden when he didn't have to. So, he'd taken to talking to her picture in his room, so that he'd have someone to talk to.

Today he'd have plenty to tell her. He could almost hear her laughing at some of the antics that them boys got into. And Oliver and his Eve, they didn't treat him like he was an old man that needed help from them. Eve had even started to call him Pop, just like Blake had since he'd been a toddler.

As he was finishing up, he was asked if he could help them through lunch if it was as busy as it had been this morning. Having nothing better to do and liking being needed, Ollie said that he would. As he was filling the pots up again, Ollie felt his grandson touch lightly on his noodle. He asked him what was up.

I have a favor to ask you. He told Adam that he'd give him the world if he could. *Thanks, Grandda, but nothing so big. But I've been asked to ask you if you'd mind giving Ivy away at the courthouse on Friday. She is nervous, I guess, about asking you, so I told her that I'd ask. I didn't think you'd have any problem with it, would you?* Ollie couldn't speak for a few seconds, his heart so filled up that he could feel it spilling from his heart by way of his tears. *Grandda?*

I'm here. I am. And I'm so plumb proud to do this for her that I can hardly stand it myself. That girl of yours, you tell her that I'm there any time she needs me. And I'd be honored to do this for the two of you. He had to pull out his handkerchief and wipe his face with it. The feelings that he had at that moment made him feel like he'd done went and won the biggest pot that there was. *I'll be there with bells on my toes, Adam. Tell her that I love her to pieces, all right?*

I will, Grandda. She's going to have her sister stand with us too. Mom is putting together a party at their house after we're married. I have to tell you, Grandda, I love this woman so very much.

Of course, you do, and I do as well. I love all them girls. I know your grandma would have too. She'd have found them all to be a hoot and would be right there egging them on in all them things they get into.

Ollie wasn't needed the entire lunch shift and made his way home.

He had a suit to get cleaned up, and he'd found some of the items she'd left for the boys. Ollie had given all the others something, the ones that were married, anyhow. She'd told him before passing away that he was to give the things to them when they found their mates. He'd plumb forgot about it with Adam.

"Love, you would just about bust if you knew what I was up to." He was sitting on his bed, her picture in his hand. "I do so miss you. But I'm going to have so much to tell you when we get together again. Them boys of ours, they sure have done this old man up proud. Come spring, I'll take you some more pictures so you can have a looksee at them."

He'd been putting pictures and other items in a tin box that he'd put on her headstone for the two of them. Instead of leaving them out there over the winter, he'd brought it home to fill as he found things. Mostly it was just little bitty things, things that someone else might think of as being silly. But he wanted to do this, and it made him feel better. Tomorrow he was going to go and see his Emma, and then he'd tell her all about the wedding when he came to see her again.

Going to find his boy Adam, Ollie found himself whistling as he made his way to him. Yes, siree, Ollie sure was a good deal happier than he had been in some time. Grandchildren, great grandchildren, and more coming all the time. This was the best thing worth living for.

Chapter 8

Adam loved the old building that had been state of the art some decades ago. It had held up well over the years but would most assuredly need some upgrades. He and Evan walked through the kitchen area, the place that would be converted into a large open area where breakfast and some light dinners would be served.

They'd decided after looking things over that it wouldn't be so much a hotel as it would be a place to relax with the family, and not have to worry about things like traffic near big highways. Nor that much in the way of crimes.

Adam walked to the counter that had served well as a front desk and sat in the only remaining chair in the place. Evan had taken the other one. Handing him his list and getting the one from his brother, they compared them to see what they were going to take care of and in what order.

"The pool can be fixed now. It's a nice one, and I've had a couple of people that I know look at the heating system in it, as well as the way it's looking. Danny and his team came out and said that the filtration system and the heater for the pool are in good shape and working. But he suggested that we might want to get the filtration part replaced soon rather than have it go out when it's most needed." Evan agreed, telling Adam that he'd take care of that first. "Good. I would also like to have the rooms enlarged. The place is nice if you only wanted to sleep here and not do anything else. The rooms are too small for even a couple, much less a family."

"I agree. The last time that Dylan and I were staying in DC, the thing that we found the most irritating was the size of the rooms. And the fact that there would only be the one bathroom. If we cut the size of the place down by half, as I was thinking, we'd have two full baths in each room. Also, there should be a couple of them that have a kitchenette. That part we both loved when we had the boys with us."

Adam wrote this down on his sheet. Evan did the same with his. Later, in a couple of days, the two of them would meet up again, this time with a more comprehensive list, and the order in which things needed to be done. This was going to be a lot of work, but in the end, both he and Evan were excited to be doing something together.

They'd bought the building several days ago. It had taken them this long to have the place cleared out of some of the more downtrodden that had taken up residency there. When they were moved on, neither one of them saw any reason to kick them to the curb. Instead, they found them a place in the shelter as well as got some of them jobs if they wanted them. Not that they'd be able to stay at the shelter for very long, not without trying to help themselves. Help was there for those that wanted it—the rest would be asked, politely, to find a job.

Evan was called out, so Adam moved around the spacious place alone. There really was a great deal that had to be done, but they both thought it was well worth the investment. Also, it would help a few people out around town. Creating jobs was one of the things that his family excelled in.

Just as he was entering the kitchen area again, Adam tried to think what would be the best way to make this area work. They had both agreed that the kitchen would be open to the public. Not to upset the diner in town. but to have more of an upper-class sort of place, where they served steaks as well as a few other items. That too would add revenue to the town. It was nice to have a place to go that didn't have too many options on the menu. Not that the diner did. It served breakfast, lunch, and dinner, but that was all the menu said. The cook, whoever was working that day, would get to pick what they had to work with. It had worked well for years, but it would be nice to have a nice sit-down type of place to go when a celebration was in mind.

He was just locking up the place, having had new locks put on, when he saw a man in the shadows of the alley between the two buildings next to his and Evan's. Not sure who it was, or for that matter what he was, Adam reached out to see if one of his family members were close when he got Sunny and David. They'd been shopping for Christmas already. He told him what he saw.

Stay right where you are. We're no more than a few blocks from you. Adam asked David how he was supposed to do that when he knew the man was still watching him. *Act like you're clumsy or something. I don't know, drop your keys and pretend to try out a few of them to lock the door.*

I'm going to be very embarrassed if this turns out to be nothing more than a man out walking his dog. David asked him if he could smell a dog and he told him no. *Actually, I don't smell anything from him. What the hell does that mean?*

Don't know, but we're coming up behind you. Turn toward me

109

when I say your name. Sunny is coming in the other side with Carter. She was coming to see you anyway about something else. I can see you.

Adam was beginning to be nervous and he hadn't any idea why. When David said his name, he turned toward him and waved back. Adam was really glad at that moment that the other man couldn't see his face. He could taste his fear of the unknown like he could hear his heart rate going up.

The gunshot startled him badly enough that he jumped. Also, and he was glad for his brother's quick thinking, he was tossed to the ground just as something streaked by him. Thinking that one of the women was hurt, he and David made their way to the alley to see what had happened.

"I didn't get any more than a shot fired off when Tanner was there and gone with the man before I could figure out what was going on." David asked Sunny if she'd been hurt. "Nah. I'm fine. But I wonder what the hell Tanner was doing here. Not to mention, out this time of the day. Do you know what his tolerance of the sun is like?"

"Pretty high. I mean, the man is as old as dirt if not more so." The clearing of a throat had them all turning to see Tanner there. Again, Adam was embarrassed and apologized to the older man. "I just didn't expect this, that's all, and it has me a little mouthy. I'm sorry."

"No need. But the threat, and that was what it was, is no longer a problem." Adam asked if he was the target. "No, it was me and my little fae that were the targets. Sadly, I will have to go to the council to tell them just what happened. The man, Randal is his name, he'd become quite the bother the way that he's been sending his minions after me."

"Are you all right then?" Tanner smiled, and Adam saw the drop of blood on his lip. Adam started to say something about it, quietly, when the old vamp licked his lip clean. Shivering once, Adam asked again if he was all right.

"I am. I promise you that I am. If not for Flora, I think that Randal might well have harmed you to make me do as he wished. The man was a fool if he thought me stupid enough not to have a good eye on him all the time." Sunny asked what Randal might have been begging for. "Me to kill him. Not really, but that is what it ended up being. I think that it would take a great deal of stupidity on another's part should they not be begging me if they tried this on whom I consider family, don't you?"

They all laughed. Tanner was a good man. and Adam knew that should he find the need to kill someone, they might as well come to Tanner and beg to make their death quick. Adam had heard about his grandda and his issues with another vamp and had it in his head since then that Tanner would take care of it soon enough.

"I have given it some thought, and I should like to purchase some land and empty places here in town as well. It is not like I need the money, but like your grandda, I find myself bored with things, and Flora and I should like to invest some time into this place." David asked him what he had in mind. "I'm not entirely sure. I do wish to help others, much as you have all helped me in one way or another. I will give that part more thought as I purchase the two buildings that are on the market by the town. Unless you have your eye on them."

"I don't think the family is in the market for anything right now. I do know that there are four houses, not very big ones, that are being shown by Josh right now. Not much in the way of buyers. He said that it was because of the winter months. I don't know."

"I'll look into those as well. I was thinking of you, David, just the other day as a matter of fact. How is your book about the Decker house coming along? I have been excited about it for some time." He told him that it was still at the editor's office, and that he expected something back in a few days. "That's wonderful. I'm sure that you did it a great deal of justice. I'm to understand that you have a great many pictures in it as well. Ollie, he told me that you have put something in the back of it to ask people if they knew anyone in the photos that you added. Brilliant idea."

David flushed with embarrassment. Adam was glad that he wasn't the only one that could be embarrassed at the drop of a hat. But as David got more confident about his work, the more alive he seemed to become. His brother was a very famous author, but Adam would bet that most people that knew David wouldn't have any idea that it was the same man that wrote the things that he did.

"So, it's going to be made into a movie? I congratulate you on that. It must be quite the feather in your family's hat to have you being so famous." David said he didn't think he'd go that far. "Nay, I would think that you'd not. But I am very proud of you, young man. You deserve this. Very much so."

"There was a gun fired." Everyone turned to him when he blurted out what he'd been thinking about. "I'm sorry. I only just realized that there was a gunshot went off. Did you have to shoot him?"

"No. But it was tempting. Randal was just pulling out his own weapon, a long beautiful sword, when I saw Tanner. The blade, I think, was for threatening you, Adam. And the gun, it was to kill you should you not have done as he wished." Adam asked Sunny how she knew that. "I touched the sword."

Sunny could touch things and know the entire history of the item by doing so. And from there, she could "track" others that had touched the person wielding the item. She was scary good at it, and Adam knew that his family had used her talent whenever they needed answers. Sunny would have gotten not just the man's intent from the blade, but also would have been able to tell who was helping him, as well as anyone that he'd killed to get what he wanted.

"Speaking of which, Tanner, there are a few others that you need to see to. Not kill—they're as innocent as kids. But they need help. Two of them, the ones that he held captive in order to change them, have died. A few more are very close to it, a botched changing from which they'll need a great deal. I don't know that they'll make it either. The will to die, it's very strong in them." Tanner said that he'd look into it now. That he needed to make arrangements to see the others of the kiss that he had inherited. "If you need assistance with them, just let us know. I can find what Dylan can't—and we both know that's not much. She's a wizard when it comes to finding things and people."

Parting from the others at the door of the hotel, Adam started for home. He had big plans for tomorrow and the next day. He was going to woo his wife. Adam loved Ivy with all his heart, and to show her how very much he did, he was going to make sure that she never regretted becoming his mate—starting with the night before they were to wed. Tomorrow night, he was going to propose to her as well, something that he should have done a while ago. Adam smiled all the way home and was thrilled when it started snowing enough to cover the ground.

Life was good. Very good, as a matter of fact.

~*~

Meghan had to wait for three more days before she'd know if she was qualified to adopt Nathan. The two of them had spent a lot of time together of late, and she loved him as much as she did her own sister. And the Whitfields had welcomed him into

113

their leap already too.

Her cell phone was ringing when she got out of the car with several bags of things for Nathan. Instead of answering it right away, she made her way into the house to greet her new staff and ask if they would bring in the last few items.

Ollie had been so wonderful to her. And when he'd found out that she was going to take Nathan into her home, the man had gone all out, even going so far as to tell her that he was as much her grandda as he was to any of the rest of them. He said that he already considered Nathan to be a great grandson as well.

Taking the phone out of her purse, Meghan looked at the unfamiliar number and decided that she'd not answer it. If they left her a message, she'd deal with it then. If not, then they'd never get in touch with her. Taking a few of the items that Nathan had requested into his room, the phone rang again.

Over the next two hours, her phone rang a total of forty times. She wasn't going to answer it after them annoying her, but it was starting to get on her last nerve even as she sat down at the sewing machine to work.

Meghan had always enjoyed sewing. But it wasn't until she had this home to go home to that she'd decided to try and make a quilt. It wasn't nearly as difficult as she'd thought it would have been. And it was decidedly more relaxing than watching the snow drift down to the ground. Or worse yet, watching the clock until it was time for Nathan to come home.

When she'd had enough, fearful of turning off the phone in the event that it was important, Meghan wrote down the number and called Adrian. He'd gotten his law degree some time ago, but she knew that his primary job, consulting, was what he had enjoyed the most. Having the information ready for him when he answered, Meghan didn't want to disrupt his day when he was sounding like he was in good humor. That was if his laughter was any indication. She started to hang up, to tell him that she butt dialed him, when he turned from humor to serious in a blink of an eye.

"What is it?" She said that it wasn't important. "Of course, it is. Tell me what has you so upset. I'm here for you, Meghan. Tell me."

She told him everything that she'd been dealing with, giving him the number when he asked as well as the times that whoever had called her. Adrian asked her a few questions. then told her that he was sending Dylan over.

"She has contacts that I can't get you. I'm trying my best to stay on the good side of the law. Sometimes that isn't as easy as it sounds, sadly." Meghan told him that she was sorry again. "Don't worry about it, my dear. I want you to call me when you're unsure of something. And even if it's harassment, I'm thinking that you aren't comfortable with that notion either."

"Why won't they leave a message if they're that hard up to talk to me? It's been going on since I arrived home earlier today. I would love to just turn it off, but I'm afraid that Nathan might need me." Adrian told her that if it had been Nathan, he would have left her a message. "True. But all I can think about is that someone has him and they want me to answer so they can tell me their demands. I don't have any money to pay a ransom, but I'll figure out something if he's in trouble. I love that boy."

"As we all do. I'm going to send Dylan your way. She's in my office now, and I'll tell her what is going on and see if she has any theories." Meghan thanked him. "I'm sure that he's all right. He has a couple of people watching him, and after we hang up, I'll talk to them as well. All right?"

"You must think I'm a silly nilly, don't you?" Adrian said that she'd been hanging out with his grandda too much and reassured her, once again, that he'd never think that of her. "Of course, you wouldn't. You and the rest of your family are about as nice as anyone I've ever had the pleasure of meeting. I'll talk to Dylan, and I'm sure that she'll tell me that I'm jumping to conclusions. I'll feel better once Nathan is home. too."

Putting her phone away, she sat on Nathan's bed and waited. She supposed that she could have called the school, asked if he'd shown up today. However, she didn't want anyone to think that she was a worrywart. Nor did she want anyone to think that she'd lost him even before getting him permanently.

Going down to the living room again, she sat at the window. It was perhaps fifteen minutes later and five more calls to her cell phone when not just Dylan, but Sunny, Carter, as well as her sister and Eve arrived. They'd been going shopping.

"We had planned to come by here anyway, to see if you'd like to go." Eve hugged her tightly, something that Meghan was beginning to enjoy very much. Her cell went off once more while she was greeting the others in much the same way. "My goodness is that this person again?"

Showing them her phone, Meghan suddenly felt drained, like she was just getting over a bad bout of flu and still needed to rest. After explaining to them what she'd been dealing with, Sunny asked if she could touch her phone. While she knew what Sunny could do, she'd never actually seen her do it. The moment that it touched her hand, Sunny swayed slightly then sat down on the couch.

Meghan wanted to cry. She'd hurt one of her friends and she felt horrific about it. Going to sit beside her, holding her hand when she asked, Meghan tried to comfort Sunny while she fought her own emotions.

"The person — or in this case, the people — that are calling you are Nathan's biological parents. They've been notified of his impending adoption by you, as well as how you are related to the Whitfield family." Meghan asked her what they wanted. "A great deal, as a matter of fact. First of all, they're seeing an attorney to find out how to go about suing you. Not that they'll ever have the chance to do so, but that's not stopping them from trying."

"I don't understand. They abandoned him, basically stripping him of his right to be in a healthy and safe environment." Sunny asked her how much she knew about the Whitfields. "Nothing much. It's not like they're any relation to me or Nathan. I mean, yes, Ollie set me up with this home. I figured that they have money. How much? I don't know. It's none of my business."

The women all looked at each other. Meghan glanced at Ivy and asked her what was going on. Of all the people in the room, she knew that her sister would tell her the truth, even if she didn't want to hear it.

"All right. The Whitfields are wealthy. I don't mean like I am, which I am a millionaire, but they have several billion dollars. Each." Meghan shook her head. "They do, Meghan. They've been investing well and taking care of their money all the way back to—I guess forever. As I said, they've invested well, bought cheap and sold high. You name it, and I'm pretty sure that they've had their hand in it concerning the market and money."

"Okay, I'm still having a hard time putting the money with these people. Not that I don't believe you. But you have to admit, they look less like billionaires than anyone I've ever seen. Not that I have a lot to do with—" She shook her head again. "I'm babbling. Another thing that I rarely do that I've only just started doing. Billionaires? Are you...and you're a millionaire? Christ, Ivy, I'm so very proud of you."

Sunny laughed, then Eve joined her. Meghan didn't know what was going on. Were they making fun of her, or were they just—?

"They're after money. These people, they've found out that Nathan is staying with me, me adopting him, and they want me to...well, the only thing that I can think of is that they want me to pay them. For, I don't know, keeping him?" Dylan told her that it was more than that, probably. "Can't we just tell them that I'm not a Whitfield? And that I don't have access to any kind of money that they're hoping that I'll give them?"

"Two things—first, they'd never believe you. Secondly, you do have access to any amount of money that you want. I don't mean for this, but for anything that you wish. The moment that Ivy became a part of the family, so did you." Meghan told her that Ollie had told her the same thing. "Then you should believe him and us. They'd drain you dry if they thought that you'd give it to them. Which, we will not."

"I'm assuming that you don't believe that they'll just give up if I don't connect with them. What will they do, kidnap Nathan and hold him until I agree to their terms? If so, then you have to know that I'd never give in to them. And if they touch one hair on his head, even to ruffle it up, then I will kick their ass all the way to the fucking rock that they slipped out from under." Sunny laughed first, then Eve. It wasn't long before they were all laughing, and it took Meghan a few minutes to figure out that they'd not been making fun of her, but of what she'd said. "What do I have to do to make them give up? I'm willing to do just about anything."

"I'm glad to hear you say that. Because I have a plan, and it'll take all of us to make it work." Meghan had always thought that Dylan was scary. All of them, as a matter of fact. But she wanted these people to realize that she wasn't one to fuck with either. "First thing you have to do is find out from Nathan what he wants to do. I honestly don't think that he'd want to go back with them, not the way that they treated them, but he has to be made aware that they're going to fight you on you adopting him. This is a decision that he must make on his own."

"I agree. And I'll talk to him as soon as he gets home. But what do I do about these calls they're making?" Carter told her that she'd have to talk to Nathan. "You think that he'll want to speak to them? Or worse yet, that he wants to go with them?"

"I don't know. I'd like to say there isn't any way, but I just don't know. Even with the fact that he doesn't know them, hardly at all as a matter of fact, there is also the fact that they are his parents." Meghan nodded, and the phone rang again. "I'd not answer any of the calls until you've talked to Nathan, as I said. Even after that, I'd not talk to them until they leave you a message. But if he wants to talk to them, I'd allow him to do so."

She didn't want to do that. It worried her to no end that they'd be able, as his parents, to talk him into whatever they wanted. Meghan was sure that her heart would shatter if he were to leave her and the rest of them. Having the little man in her life had given her more hope and happiness than she'd had in a very long time.

Meghan had decided that she'd tell him what she knew, not showing any emotion at all, and let him come to his own decision. As soon as he got off the bus, it was all planned out. She had written and destroyed several ways to tell him about his parents.

But, as usual, nothing worked out the way she wanted it to. As soon as she saw him, Meghan lost control of her tightly held sorrow. Babbling it all to him, what they knew for sure and what that would do to him should he have his parents back in

119

his life, Nathan held her tightly as he too cried.

"I'll let you do as you wish. I'm not saying that I won't miss you terribly, but they're your parents, and that's all that you should think about. I won't ask or beg you to stay. This is for you to decide, not me." Nodding, Nathan held her, not saying anything. "I'll let you think on it. And I want you to know, I will support you in anything you wish to do."

Chapter 9

Ivy was exhausted. She'd had three back to back surgeries last night well into early this morning, and she wasn't sure that she could hold a fork in her hand to feed herself, she was that tired. Standing under the spray in the bathroom, Ivy leaned against the wall, letting the warm water rain down over her body. It wasn't until someone said her name that she realized that at some point she'd dozed off while standing up.

"Ivy are you all right?" She didn't recognize the voice but knew that it had to be Adam. He'd called her earlier, just as she was closing up her last patient, and asked if he could do anything for her. "I brought you some breakfast and some hot tea from home. There is also a bag of apples and some juice cups here. Will you come out and eat?"

"Yes. I'm coming. I have to check on my patient, but I'll be able to eat after that." He told her that Evan was doing that, and that he was going home right after. "He's so sweet. The car accident, did he tell you about it?"

Now she was drying off, her hair wrapped up in a large towel. Twice she had to remember if she'd brushed her teeth or not, and went ahead and did it anyway. Now she was debating if she could curl up under the sink and sleep until she didn't hurt any more.

Adam came into the spacious room with her and sat on the commode while she tried to run a brush through her hair. Ivy was seriously tired. Not since she'd been in her last year of her residency had she felt like this. When he took the brush from her and sat her on the counter, Ivy leaned into him while he helped her get put together.

"I know you don't like to know the names of the people you work on, so we'll just have them numbered. Okay?" Nodding, she didn't say anything as he hypnotically ran his fingers over her skull. "Number one is in intensive care but doing much better than expected. He is still on the vent, but Evan doesn't think that he'll be there for much longer." When she nodded, he picked her up in his arms after finishing with her hair. "Number two has to be transferred to a bigger hospital that can care for his type of injury. The medic that was riding with him to OSU told Evan that the man had coded twice, and he didn't expect him to make it there. Evan said that he'd let you know what happened after you got some rest. What happened to him?"

"A drunk driver took a turn too quickly and smashed the family's car into a sidewalk full of people. Seven were killed, counting two children on the crosswalk and the family in the car. The drunk, of course, walked away without a scratch. The family of the man that we worked on were all killed because of him. Because instead of plowing into the sidewalk, he turned to avoid the children and put himself in the line of a semi-truck. The driver of the truck died too." She looked at the food all laid out on her desk. "I'm so tired."

"Number three didn't make it." She nodded—she would feel the pain of it later. As soon as she was on his lap, he picked up the fork and started filling it with the foods that she loved. "I have it on good authority that the drunk driver is going to prison. A friend of mine that works at the station said that he's being charged with seven murders, and that he was going be spending a lot of time in prison. Number three, as I said, didn't make it, but you'd prepared her family for that, so they are upset and devastated, but taking it better than anyone thought they would."

"She was too heavy. And since she wasn't doing much to take care of her weight or her diabetes, she didn't stand a chance."

"Evan said that he'd been telling her and her family for years that she needed to drop the weight. I guess you had as well." She nodded and moaned when he put mashed potatoes and gravy in her mouth. "I've spoken to Meghan. She wanted me to tell you that she and Nathan have spoken about what is going on with his parents, and that he wants nothing to do with them. But, I'm to tell you that he's going to talk to them. Meghan wanted me to thank you for telling her that would be better for them both."

"He might change his mind later, and it wouldn't do her a bit of good if he thought that she was keeping him from them — or worse yet, that she had lied to him about any of this." When he pushed the plates away, she realized that she'd eaten all the food. "You're too good to me, you know that, don't you? I wouldn't have done any of this for you."

"Yes, you would have. But you would have made me feed myself and been a bully about it. How are you feeling right now, babe?" She told him that she hurt. "Yes. I talked to Evan. He said that you did such a wonderful job in the operating room that he almost forgot a couple of times that he was a doctor too. Said that you put him to shame in there."

"I very much doubt he would allow me to put him to shame. He's a glory hog, did you know that?" Adam pointed out that he'd grown up with Evan, so he knew that he could be selfish when there was praise handed out. "He's a dream to work with. I've enjoyed it a great deal. Your brother is good at what he does too. Don't let him tell you any differently."

She must have dozed off. When she woke, Adam was holding her in his arms and sleeping too. Moving so as not to wake him, she got up and stretched. Adam laughed when she bent at the waist and touched her toes.

"Are you terribly tired?" Turning to glance at him, Ivy had to smile. The man was a wonder to her. He could bring her out of her bad mood when one struck her, or he could make her feel like the sexiest woman in the world with just the sound of his voice. "You keep looking at me like that and we'll never make it home. And I have such plans for you when we get there."

"Like what sort of plans? Are you going to make me scream out your name? Perhaps make me beg for more? What kind of things are you going to do to me?" Adam laughed and told her that she was a selfish lover. "You have no idea. I'd like nothing more than to sit on your naked cock and ride you until neither of us can walk."

He unbuttoned his pants and pulled on the zipper slowly. Ivy's mouth watered when he moved them down further on his thighs and stroked his cock through his boxers. It was the most frustrating and erotic thing she'd ever seen. Turning around to face him, she began telling him what she wanted to do to him while she too removed her clothing.

"You are going to scream out my name several times before I come myself. That's the plan at least. You have a way about you that makes me melt when you touch me. My skin feels like it's on fire when you blow your breath over me. And when you eat me, I cannot think beyond letting my body do what you want it to." He pushed his boxers down over his cock, the tip leaking so badly now that she finished stripping and got down on her knees. "The thought of tasting you, having you fill my mouth, makes me so wet, Adam, that I could easily come right now, without you even touching me."

Kissing just the tip of his engorged cock, she nearly came when he moaned, some of his warm liquid sliding across her lips as she licked him around the crown. Each sound that he made, every time he rose his hips up for her to take him deeper, Ivy felt her pussy gush with her cream, so much so that she had to touch herself for some relief, no matter how unfulfilling it was.

"Take me into your mouth, love. I want to feel what fire feels like. I want to fuck your mouth like I'm going to do your pussy. Then when I'm ready, I'm going to pull from your luscious mouth and cover your face and breasts with myself." She moaned, her body on fire for what he said to her. And when she looked up at him, his cock in her mouth, she swallowed him down past the tightness of her throat.

Nothing could have prepared her for the feeling of him filling her mouth and her throat. She cried out around his cock, making him scream out her name over and over as he came.

Adam held her head to him, fucking her hard enough that she knew that her throat would be tender tomorrow. But she didn't care — she loved this man, and no matter what he did to her, she'd gladly take it.

When he pulled from her mouth and tossed her to the floor onto her back, Adam went from male to cat in seconds. And when he clamped his sharp teeth into her belly, she screamed out not in climax, but in sickening pain. When she thought that she could take no more, he bit her hard into her shoulder. The

125

bones breaking there had her sick with it. Ivy turned her head away and threw up on the carpet.

Dizzy now with pain, she felt him bite her thigh. At this point she wasn't sure that she could have felt anything. The pain all over her body was too much to bear. Just as she was slipping into unconsciousness, she heard Adam telling her over and over how sorry he was. Ivy put her hand onto his large head as he deepened the bite at her thigh.

"It's all right. I'm all right." Ivy wasn't sure that she was, but he was so upset that she couldn't tell him that she thought for sure that she was going to die. "I love you so much, Adam. More than I think that my heart can hold at times."

This time when she was sick, there was nothing left on her belly. Blood pooled at her navel, and her heart started to slow a little more with each beat. When her hand slipped from his head, she didn't have the strength to lift it back up again and closed her eyes. Ivy loved Adam. And whatever he'd done to her just now, she knew that he'd never meant for her to hurt so badly. Then, closing her eyes, she was sure that she was dead, and she told him once again how very much she loved him.

~*~

Adam knew that his cat had to do this to her. He just wished that he would have listened to Evan and held off for a little while longer. They were to be married in the morning, and she was going to be very pissed at him because she wasn't going to be up to making it. And his mom and dad would kill him. Christ, he was terrified.

He'd never changed anyone before. Not ever. While he knew that it was painful on the other half, there was also a slim chance that they wouldn't survive it. When his cat let go of her leg, then himself, Adam held Ivy in his arms while rocking her back and forth.

"I'm sorry, love. I should have had more control over what he wanted. My cat loves you so much — so do I — but we both should have waited until we were wed, don't you think?" He laughed a little. "You're going to kick my ass when you wake up. And I'm going to let you. Although, I think that you'd do it anyway and make a good showing of putting me in my place, when I'm just sitting here whining like a big baby."

Wrapping her up in the blanket that was lying across the back of the couch, he laid down with her and held her tightly to him. Adam wasn't going to leave her, not now but he also didn't want his family around. He loved them, but this, to him, was a private time between the two of them. It wasn't until Dylan contacted him through their link that he remembered that he should have asked her permission before doing this.

Is Ivy all right? He told her that she was resting and that he was sorry. *Don't be. I'm glad you did it. She's not in any kind of danger with this happening to the two of you. But I'm sure that sometime she'll be thrilled to death later that you changed her. When she wakes up, let me know and we'll have a large party.*

Do you realize that she's the first mate to come to us without any bad guys after her? And that she has all the issues that she might have had taken care of long before we met? Dylan laughed. *I hope she finds what I've done to her just as funny as you think it is now.*

She will. You have a very intelligent mate there, Adam. I do hope that you tell her how lucky you are to have her every day. He promised her that he would. *Good. I do have some news for you. Nathan's parents are in the local B&B. I'd like for you to also think about having that place that you and Evan are working on up and running soon. There are two more mates coming. And if the mates come here and the bad guys after them need a place to stay, perhaps we can get rid of them in our own setting and not mess up the bed and breakfast.*

When she closed the connection, Adam thought about what she'd said. He wasn't sure if she was kidding or not, talking about getting rid of the people that may or may not come after them. Adam had a feeling that she was serious, but he didn't want to think about that. It was hard to tell sometimes with Dylan. Closing his eyes while holding onto Ivy, he decided that he wasn't going to ask her. He thought it would be better if he didn't know.

Waking up on the couch, Adam felt his body had stiffened up, and his arms were sore as well. Looking around, he noticed the note standing up on Ivy's desk with his name on it. Standing and stretching, Adam only just then realized that Ivy was a cat. And she had gotten up already—she'd not had to rest up for several days as others he'd heard about had. Christ, he loved that woman.

Picking up the note, he could smell her on it. Her cat was right there where he could catch her scent. Opening the folded paper, he was hit harder with her scent. It was so delicate, so amazingly her, that he felt his cock stretch and harden.

So, I'm a tiger. I love you for this. I was terrified that I was going to die, but I so love that you and your pretty kitty helped me be safer. Laughing, he sat down at her desk to finish the note. *I'm on call until noon today. The emergency department is so short-staffed right now, I have some feelers out for some of my old gang to come out to be interviewed. I've spoken to Evan about it. Anyway, I thought that if I had stayed there with you all wrapped around me, I wouldn't have been able to leave you. I'm in the ER when you wake up. I love you dearly. Oh, before I forget, your mom is a saint, just so you know. She has everything set up for us to get hitched anytime we have a few minutes. I hope you don't mind.*

Putting the note down on the desk again, Adam leaned back in her chair. It was a very stark room. No pictures or diplomas were on the wall. He knew that she'd lost a great many things with the fire, but he also knew that she'd not bother getting a copy of any of it. Picking up his phone, wanting to make her space just for her, he made several phone calls and got everything that he wanted for her lined up. Leaving the office then, making sure that the door was locked, Adam made his way to the emergency department.

He found Ivy talking to a couple. The woman he thought he knew. It was difficult to tell with her being covered in so much blood. The man, hurt as well, held the woman next to him as she sobbed. Ivy told them several times that she was sorry for the decision they had to make at this moment, and for the bad news she was imparting to them. Adam didn't know what was going on, but he knew that he couldn't talk to her right now.

Standing next to the desk at the front of the department, Adam asked Linda what was going on. She shook her head and wiped at her nose as she looked at the couple.

"They were in an accident. Their little boy, about four, was ejected from the car even though he was buckled in the proper way." Adam asked if he had been killed. "No, but things just don't look that good for him. His momma found him a few yards from the impact. Dad was unconscious when he was pulled from the wreckage. Doctor Ivy is telling them their options. Which, sadly, aren't all that good."

When Ivy moved toward the desk, he started to reach for her when she shook her head. She gave orders to Linda, telling her to make sure that they could spend as much time as they wished with their son, and to call her if there was any change in the next several hours.

Ivy took his hand and took him to the doctors' lounge, and then nearly collapsed when they were behind closed doors. She cried harder than he'd ever seen her do, and Adam was at a loss

129

at to what to do for her. Holding her seemed so little when he could feel her suffering like it was his own.

Ivy looked up at him and his heart broke for her. Her face was puffy from the tears — the sorrow there had him picking her up and holding her on his lap. When she finally spoke, Adam having given her time to do so, she spilled out the story that had him wanting to go and find the man responsible for the accident and killing him again.

"He had just been buckled into his seat to go to the zoo when the car driven by an idiot came out of nowhere and hit theirs hard enough that it went through a stoplight and into oncoming traffic." Adam asked her where the parents had been. "The mother was just opening the door to enter the car, and the father was on the other side, where the impact occurred, to get in as well. Neither of them made it inside, but the mother was knocked into the car next to it. The father, a shifter, was thrown into the woods beyond the parking lot of the restaurant they'd been coming out of."

He'd seen his brother be devastated by such horrors of his job. Evan would hurt for days before he was able to get a good grip on his emotions after losing a patient. He would wear his pain like armor sometimes, especially when a child was involved. Evan had told him once that he wished that he could save all the children from those like the one from today, but he knew also that it was a fact of life that people were stupid for the most part. And it seemed that children were the ones that took the brunt of their foolhardiness.

When Ivy left him, Adam made his way out to the front desk again. Linda informed him that the child had died and that his parents had been with him when he had. Nodding, he hurt for them too. And although he didn't have children of his own, he had brothers who did, and he didn't know what he'd do if anything happened to their children.

About an hour later, Adam helped out by fielding calls. Most of it was just talking to someone in a certain room, and Linda showed him how to transfer calls. But there were times when he didn't know much more than the callers did. Those calls he had to send to another department. Someone there would have to give them information.

He saw Evan twice when he was called in, Ivy every hour or so. He'd not been surprised to see his grandda coming in. The man knew more people and their families than anyone. He came in and made his rounds before having a seat with he and Linda.

By the time Ivy was off duty, he was drained. He couldn't imagine how anyone did this job over the extent of their lives without having to seek professional help. The things that he'd never realized, the way things were done, Adam thought for sure that he'd stay a farmer until his dying day rather than have to do a job that for the most part was depressing. Adam wanted to do something fun, something that would take both their minds, mostly Ivy's, off their day.

Walking out into the fresh snow, feeling the bite of the cold, Adam wanted to see Ivy's cat. He knew that she'd be beautiful, also that she'd be unique. Taking her hand in his, noticing that she hadn't bundled up to leave the hospital, Adam took her to the back side of the hospital, where there was a walking path. Taking off his shirt, he let his cat take him, knowing that this was just what they both might need.

Shift. Ivy told him that she wasn't sure that she was ready for that. *Sure you are. But if you don't want to, then run.*

Ivy stared at him for several long tense minutes. And when she smiled and took off running, Adam heard her laughing. Yes, he decided, this was just what the doctor ordered. Taking off after her, he noticed that her shoe prints had turned into paws. Stopping, his need to run her down stilled for a moment, Adam looked for Ivy in the perfectly laid out landscape. When he spotted her, Adam sat in the snow to enjoy her figuring herself out.

I can see why you love this. I'd be a cat all the time if I could. Adam told her that she'd soon grow bored with it. *No, I don't think so. I feel stronger, more alive than I did before. It's like, not only am I this different being, I'm also magical. You must think that I'm a sap.*

On the contrary. I'm enjoying seeing the freshness that you've brought to being a cat. I've been one my entire life, done just what you've done today countless times. Yes, I can see your feeling this way. He went to her, walking slowly as she played and romped in the snow. *You're so beautiful, love. The most beautiful tiger I've ever seen. And I love you with all my heart.*

The two of them played for nearly an hour. Adam could have gladly stayed out here forever, but he knew that they both had obligations. Family, their jobs—all things that made this right now seem like the best medicine. He took the time to show her things that she could do now, as well as stuff that she had to do to keep herself and those around her safe.

When they were ready to go home, Adam gave Ivy the bag of clothing that he had stashed in his truck and let her pick from it first. He had to laugh when he suggested that they just go home like they were. Ivy told him to behave. Adam decided right then and there that he was going to do this more often.

When the planting and harvesting time of the year came around, he rarely took the time to shift and relax. Adam rarely had a meal on time, much less resting. It was then that he came to a profound decision. He was going to take more time, not just in minutes here and there, but doing it daily, and with Ivy.

He'd been doing it for so long, putting it off, that he was never bothered by it any longer. Now, with Ivy, he thought that he would miss it more.

Adam was glad now that his grandda had come by to see him. He'd not told him that he'd already been thinking about asking him to go with him when he went to find a ring for Ivy. But when he'd given him Grandma's ring to give to Ivy, Adam knew that she'd treasure it as much as he did her. And tomorrow, if all went well, they'd be married.

"What are you thinking about so hard?" Adam couldn't help it, he wiggled his brows at her. "Behave yourself. Men and sex. I mean, you're really good at it, but that seems to be all that you think about."

"Of course it is. As you've pointed out, I'm a man." She just sighed heavily, and he had to laugh again. "Actually, what I was thinking about was something that my grandda wanted to see me about recently. He gave me my grandma's rings. The second set of them that he purchased for her long ago."

"That's lovely he bought her more than one set of rings. I don't know if you realize this or not, but you have a very romantic grandda. Your dad is as well. I've never seen your mom without something new that Oliver has gotten her. They're a wonderful couple." Adam pulled out the wedding set and handed it to her, box and all. "Oh, Adam. These are beautiful. And so well done."

"Grandda has his hands in a great many things, which brings him into contact with a lot of talented people. Anyway, he had this one made for her just after my dad started school, Grandda told me that she was inconsolable when he walked to school. In order to make her smile, just a bit, he went to his buddy and had this made for her." Ivy told him that was very romantic. "You would think that would keep him from getting into trouble for a little while. But not only did she get upset with him a few minutes later when he brought home a dog for my dad, but she also fussed at him about nearly everything else after that. Grandda got into more trouble with Grandma, he told me, just to see that fire in her eyes. Grandda is a card, as my grandma used to call him."

Taking the little box back, he took the engagement ring out first. Slipping the wedding band and box back into his pocket, Adam took Ivy's hand into his. Sliding the ring onto her finger, Adam wasn't the least bit surprised to see that it fit her like a glove.

Kissing the back of her hand, then turning it over to kiss her palm, Adam looked directly into her eyes. My God, she was beautiful. Holding her hand in his, Adam cleared his throat. Love rolled over him. No, that wasn't the right word. It took him like a storm how much he loved her.

"Ivy Dawn Walton, will you marry me? Please? Words fail me on how you make me feel. How I can tell you how much I love you. You would make me the happiest man in the world if you were to consent to marrying me and making an honest man of me." Before he'd allow her to answer him, Adam kissed her quickly. "I would love to have as many children as you want. And so long as you're happy, I couldn't care less what sex they were. But I would love to have myself a daughter with you. And for her to be just like you."

"I will. Oh Adam, I will marry you and be happy with you too."

Adam kissed her again, this time showing her as best he could how much he loved her. He knew that life would never be boring with Ivy. Excited for the next stage in their life, he and she made love all through the night and well into the next morning and were nearly late for their own wedding.

Chapter 10

Nathan wasn't sure what to think about his parents. They'd abandoned him — by his way of thinking, not once but twice. Doing some reading in old newspapers, there had only been a few references about his disappearance in the months after he'd gone missing. After that, he'd found out from talking to a reporter, the incident was republished on his birthday every year. And every year, the reporter told him, his parents couldn't be reached for comment on how they were dealing with it. Nathan didn't know why, but he didn't think they'd been *dealing* with anything. Only, as he'd overheard Meghan say to her sister, that they'd been just as happy to have him gone as she was to have him in her life.

Meghan was a really super person. She made him laugh. Made sure that he had what he needed, and sometimes what he didn't need. When she'd signed him up for school to start the week after Thanksgiving, Nathan and her had gone out and gotten him new shoes, clothes, as well as his very first backpack.

"Nathan?" He had zoned out for a moment. but she didn't make him feel stupid over it. She never made him feel stupid

135

about things that he did. "They're here. It's not too late for us to reschedule this if you'd like."

"No, I'm okay. I just want to see what they want." When she sat down in the chair that she kept hopping up and down in, he smiled at Meghan. She was more nervous than he was, he thought. "You promise not to leave me with them? I don't think that they'll hurt me or anything, but I might need you there."

"No, I won't leave you. And you're aware that Adrian is going to be there, right? He's just going to be there to answer any questions you might have in this." He nodded. "And the rest of the family, our family, they're going to be there as well. Just in the event that you need them."

"I'm glad. Aren't you?" She nodded, and Nathan felt his heart hurt for what this was doing to her. "We'll be fine, Meghan. I know it."

Although he'd already decided to not go with his parents, he'd promised Meghan that he'd not make the decision officially until he talked to them. He no more trusted them than a snake in a room full of tasty rats. Nathan thought of Grandda Ollie and had to smile. Some of the things he said were just too funny not to repeat. And there were a few that he wasn't allowed to repeat.

"I want you to know that wherever you hang your hat, I'm still going to be here for you whenever you need me. And if'n the people that created you say that you can't see me no more, then I want you to know that all you have to do is pick up that phone of yours and call me. I'll be there lickety split for you." Nathan hugged the elderly man, trying to hide his tears from him. "You're a good boy, Nathan. And a good hearted one too. You'll be fine. I know it."

But how did anyone know if he'd really be fine or not? He'd been thinking about it a lot, and he had a feeling that his parents were only out for one thing. Money.

Nathan knew that the Whitfields had money. A great deal of it, Meghan had told him. And while they were generous with it, helping others with it when they needed it, they were never stupid about it. Nathan had already figured out, even in the short time that he'd been with them, that his parents were terrible with money and not at all generous, especially when it didn't give them more.

When his name was called to go into the courtroom, he stood up and adjusted his tie. Dylan had told him it was always good to put your best foot forward in this sort of thing. It wasn't exactly what she'd said. Nathan knew better than to repeat anything she might say. She sure did have a way with words, he thought.

The judge wasn't sitting at the big desk that he'd seen on television when there had been one to watch. Instead, he was sitting at a table with just a plain suit on, and no robe or anything like that. When he was asked to have a seat, Nathan sat as far from Welham and Evelyn as he could. Under the table, he reached for and gripped Meghan's hand tightly. He had to admit, he was as afraid as he'd ever been in his life.

"Hello, Nathan. My name is Judge Wicker. We're here today to talk to you about your feelings on things left unsaid about your—"

"Those people have no right taking him right from under our watch. He's our son, not the famous Whitfields'." Nathan looked at Evelyn. He wouldn't call her mom, nor the man that had fathered him dad. They weren't here for anything but what they could get. Even if he'd not overheard someone say that about them, he would have been able to figure it out. "We want to press charges against them and have them pay for the trouble that they put us through."

137

"And what sort of trouble have they put you through, Mrs. Hitchcock? Did they rough you up to take him? Did they, I don't know, drop him off at the hospital, telling all the staff that could hear them that they didn't think they could raise him to be their own? I wonder what you might have said had the woman that took him in the first place perhaps killed him." The judge looked at Nathan. "As I was saying when I was rudely interrupted, we're here to see what it is that you wish to do."

"He's just a kid. What sort of things do you suppose he'd say? I'm sure that he has his own stuff that they bought for him. Probably a car too, even though he's only ten." Nathan told Wilhelm that he was actually twelve. "Whatever. I'm sure that he's been promised the moon if he'd say that he didn't want to be with us."

"I do have a lot." He looked at the judge when Wilhelm said he knew it. "I have a roof over my head that I don't have to worry about leaking on my face. There is always hot water, no matter what time I take a shower. My clothing is new and not full of holes, and I even get to go to school like other kids. But the best part of all is that nobody is tying me to the floor or making me help steal from other people that no more deserved it than I did being dropped off like I was bath water on a Saturday night."

Judge Wicker laughed and it reminded him of the Santa he'd seen in the big mall in Columbus. Nathan smiled back at him. He really liked having something to laugh about.

"I'm guessing that you've been spending a lot of time with Ollie Whitfield. He's a good man. He told me just this morning that he is going to have you call him Grandda no matter how this turns out." Nathan said that he loved the old man. "Yes, I can see that you do. There are a great many people in this town that love him as well."

138

"They've been really good to me, sir. Meghan and her sister told me that so long as I was alive, I'd have a safe home. I didn't know how much I needed that until someone gave it to me." Nathan looked at the family, his family should he want it. "If it's all the same to you, sir, I'd like to stay with them. They're g—"

"You ungrateful cur." Nathan looked at his father, Welham, when he stood up and shouted at him. It was then that he noticed that the entire group of Whitfields, all of them, stood up as well. "You think you just say what you want to do? I'll tell you the answer to that. You can't. Your mother and I, we grieved for a long time for you being gone. Nobody came to give us any information. They didn't look very hard, if you ask me. Now you just show up out of the blue, and that was hard on us. I don't know if you even know what we went through to get you back and all."

"Your Honor, if you'd not mind, I have a few things that I can add to Mr. and Mrs. Hitchcock's claim about what they'd been through. Or in their case, what they're claiming to not have gotten. I do believe that once you've heard this, you'll be able to make a better judgement in this case." Wilhelm started shouting at Dylan as soon as she spoke, telling her to keep her mouth shut, that she had nothing to do with anything. "Oh, but I do. And if you tell me to shut up again, I will rip your tongue out of your throat and wipe your ass with it."

Nathan wasn't sure that she wouldn't do it anyway. He really liked Dylan, but like everyone in the family, he was a little afraid of her. She was as bad-assed as anyone he'd ever come across since being taken from his home all those years ago.

When given permission to approach the bench, Nathan looked at his biological parents. Since he'd been living with

Meghan, he could now see what wealth could give a person. And from the looks of the two of them, they looked like they had some too.

He had no recollection of his family before recently. Had someone asked him, he might have not remembered his last name. Shelby had called him Moron for most of his life, and for a while there, he'd thought that it was his middle name or something like that.

Shelby was going to prison, and for a long time. He'd not been the only kid that she'd taken, and had she not messed with the Whitfields, he was as sure as he could be that he'd not have been the last. Shivering once, he went back to his thoughts on the two that had brought him into the world.

The day that he'd seen them for the first time that he could remember, he thought that Evelyn had turned her nose up at him. And now that he'd been observing them for a couple of days, he knew now that Welham had been angry. At what, he'd had no idea, until he spoke with the police. Not only had Sunny been with him, as well as Adrian for legal representation, but so had Ollie. Now that was a man that he'd love to be related to.

"I'm going to ask you some questions about your stay with Ms. Crock. All right?" Nathan had glanced at the three people that had come to mean a great deal to him. When they nodded, he told Dale Winston, the sheriff, that he was ready. "Good. You're a very lucky young man. I need to tell you that right from the start. And what I mean by that will become clearer as we talk."

"Am I in trouble?" The man had told him that he wasn't. "I can answer your questions. But I don't know how much I can help you. I'm just glad to have found Adam in the first place. They've all been good to me since I was taken to his house."

"Yes, you are lucky to have found them. Now, the time

140

that you spent with Ms. Crock, were there any other children around? Not necessarily your age, but younger. Sometimes babies? I'm just fishing for answers here, not trying to upset you." Nathan had no idea why asking him questions about others would upset him, but he nodded. "Do you by any chance know what happened to them? I mean, they weren't with you when you made it to Adam's house, correct? What I'd like to know is if you can tell me where they might be."

"There were some babies. I watched them when Shelby went on her runs. I don't know what that meant, but when she came back, she had money. They never stayed with me for very long. Just a few days to a week." He thought of something, then looked at Sunny again. "Some of them had name bracelets on them, like the one I had on me when I was in the hospital. I wrote them down. I was going to go and see them if I ever got out, and see how they were doing. I can give those to you if you want. I would write them down on this little book I'd taken once. I was.... Never mind. I stole a book and wrote them with a pen the bank was handing out at this fair thing."

"You're very brave, Nathan. And if you tell me where you took the book from, I'll make sure that he understands that you will close a great many cases with the information you stashed away." He thanked her and told her where the book was. "Do you know which church it was? I mean, there are four on Main Street alone. If you can't remember, that's fine too. I can find it."

Nodding, he turned back to Dale. He had had the strangest smile on his face. Ignoring it, he told him the names of the children that he could remember. Also, since he'd kept most of them, he told him where the baby's bracelets were.

When he was finished talking to the police officer, he had to go to his room. Nathan felt his skin crawl, and took a long hot shower to try and wash off the feeling that he'd been dipped in something nasty. The things that they'd told him, the information that they'd been able to figure out, made him doubly glad that he'd not been left to stay with his parents, the biological ones, because he was sure that he might not have survived it.

And now here he sat with all the people that had been so nice to him, so supportive that he felt his heart lighten, his mind clear up. Nathan couldn't have picked out better people to be around, and he was thrilled for it.

~*~

Adrian had read the contents of the paperwork that had been handed to Judge Wicker. Every few minutes he looked at the couple that was suing Adam and Meghan. They'd not mentioned Ivy, because apparently they'd not known about her. Which was fine by him. Adrian wanted this done yesterday. Not only because he wanted justice, but because he hated to be in the same room with them.

"I'm going to call a short recess. Don't anyone leave, if you want to hear this thing through, I'm not going to take that long." Pounding his gavel down on the desk that he was sitting at, James Wicker left them all there without another word.

Adrian knew that it was going to be only the few minutes that he'd promised everyone. Sunny and the rest of the family had been working nonstop on the paperwork, and they'd provided so many phone numbers to verify things that Adrian was sure this was going to be a win for him and the rest of the family. The Hitchcocks were in for a big awakening when this was done.

Adrian didn't look around the room. He wanted to, badly. But he wanted to look like a man that had not one care in the world. He'd been practicing that for the last several months, since it had been pointed out to him that he could be read like a book.

"If you were to look at a group of your own people like you're looking now, they'd be scared too. Perhaps scared isn't the right word, but they'd feed off what you're showing, and that could be bad. The country doesn't want to see that their president is afraid or untrusting." He'd told Henry that he was scared. "Yes, I'm sure you are. But, and this is the funny part, you don't show it as much as you used to. Keep working on your facial expressions and you'll be fantastic when it comes to meetings."

Adrian worked on that now as he waited for the judge to come back. Every once in a while it would hit him that he was the governor of the state of Ohio, and that he was getting more and more people telling him what a good job he was doing in just using his hometown to see how to make things work.

The school had all new play equipment, and most of the cost had come by way of donations. Three more cities around his little town were implementing things as he had. The library was getting new shelving. Programs were being set up to help with after school sitting for working parents.

The one that he was most proud of was the lunch program. Like a lot of cities in all states, there was some grumbling and complaints from parents about what their children were being fed. He'd had a meeting with the parents of the children, as well as the school board, and had volunteers coming in daily to not only help with serving, but also making the meals for the kids.

Adrian laughed to himself. Of course, since doing that, there had been less complaints about anything. Because as soon as they opened their mouths to bitch about things, he'd just shove the volunteer list in front of them and tell them that they should help in whatever area they found lacking. That had been his mom's idea, and it shut them up quickly, complimenting him after that for a good job. Most people, he'd come to realize, would rather shut up than to pony up, as Grandda was fond of saying.

The nudge to his arm had him look at Nathan. He'd really fallen for the kid. He was smart, savvy, and he knew the meaning of being kicked to the curb more than most. Nathan could have come out of this as a bitter person. But Adrian had noticed that he was hanging out more with Kyle and Elliot, Dylan and Evan's boys, and becoming a good hand at the ranch. Adam had hired him for the fall work, which wasn't all that much, so he could have some money of his own.

Standing when told, Adrian and the state appointed attorney for the Hitchcocks were asked to approach the judge. When Sunny spoke to him, he sort of zoned out from the judge and listened to her. She was laughing hard, but once she told him what was going to happen, he had to hide his own smile.

Listen to the judge. I'll talk with you later. Oh, and by the way, you're welcome. He asked her what she'd done. *Nothing. But by Nathan giving me what he did, I was able to find all the children. They were sold on the black web. I'll talk to you later.*

James looked pissed. More than that, he looked murderous. It wasn't often that this man got into a temper, but right now, he'd bet anything that the man would gladly have put the Hitchcocks before a firing squad. And more than likely would have pulled the trigger himself.

"Mr. and Mrs. Hitchcock, you are going to be remanded over to a higher court today. You'll be sitting in a cell, not much larger than you had that poor boy locked away in." Welham started to complain but James cut him off with a bang to the desk. Not even with the gavel. "You will keep your tongue behind your teeth, or so help me, I'll have you sitting in a prison

144

with all sorts of deviants. Now, as I was saying before being so rudely interrupted. You're being charged with — let me get this all straight here. You know, this is just too long to say it all today. I'd like to go home and shower, to get the stench of you two off my skin. I'm ashamed to have you residing in the same state as myself. You sold your son to that woman. Have you any idea what he suffered because of that? How much he had to endure because you didn't want him? Christ, you people are dangerously stupid."

"We didn't do that." James just cocked his brow at Evelyn when she spoke up. "You have no idea what we had to go through when that woman took our little boy. And now these people are trying to turn him away from us. They're the ones that should be behind bars. I don't know where you've gotten your information, but it's all lies."

"Really? Well, once she was talked to, Ms. Crock told us all about your little deal with her. You'd kidnap babies from the hospital and sell them to her for a tidy profit. And if that wasn't bad enough, you'd tell them which houses to rob. And by putting that young man inside the home by illegal means, the three of you would again share in the profits." He looked around the room, and then asked Nathan to stand up. "I'm so sorry, young man, that you've been put through all this. If there is anything I can do to help you, you just let me know. I'll make sure that you have my number too."

"Your Honor? If you're really serious about that, I know what you can help me with." James glanced at Adrian, then back at Nathan. "Meghan, Ms. Walton, said that I could be her kid. And all the Whitfields, they're really good to me too. I have a backpack of my own. And friends that I don't have to worry about having to take from them. I have food when I want it, as well as Meghan giving me hugs whenever I want them.

Sometimes even when I'm not sure that I want one."

Meghan stood up along with all the other members of the family when James asked her to do so. James laughed, telling her that she had a good support system. She assured him that she did, and that she did want to adopt Nathan.

"She will do no such thing." Adrian looked at Evelyn. "I don't know where you got all these lies from, but that woman is not going to take our son from us. Not without a price, anyway. We're going to need a better lawyer than this person here. And then there will be compensation for dragging us through this when we had nothing to do with it. If they want him, it's going to cost them. They seemed to have all the money anyway."

No one said a word. She had just offered to sell her child in front of a sitting judge. Adrian turned to Meghan and asked her to take Nathan into the hall. This, he had a feeling, was about to get nasty quickly.

As soon as he was gone, Adrian turned to James.

"Where is my money, big boy?" Adrian told her that there wouldn't be any coming. "You think so? Well, I got news for you. He's my son, and I will do whatever I want with him. By damned if I won't. I'm sick to death of people thinking that we're the bad guys right now. You'll either pay up, or I'll have him killed right in front of you."

A threat. She'd just threatened a person in a government position. Adrian didn't even look at James. He could only hope that the man was hearing what he was. That they didn't give two shits about Nathan except in a way that could make them money.

James stood up, and no one in the room could believe what was transpiring right in front of them. When he made his way to the steps, he yelled for the bailiff to come and take the couple away. The two of them were screaming about money and how

146

they were being victimized over this, and that everyone was out to get them. Adrian didn't have any idea where that notion had come from with these two, but he was glad to have this day over.

Within two hours, not only was Nathan free of his parents, he also gained an entire family. Meghan kept hugging him, telling Adrian how much she appreciated him stepping in for them. He hadn't, not really. All he'd done was sit with Nathan while everything seemed to have been worked out for him. Nathan was beside himself with happiness too.

"I wanted to tell you thanks, Uncle Adrian. I thought for sure they were going to take me with them when we were all done today." Adrian told him that was never going to happen. "I know you say that, but I don't really trust much. I'm getting there—you guys are making it easy for me to do that too."

"You're a good person, Nathan, that has had a shitty life so far. But you're going to be all right now, I think. Don't you?" Nathan grinned and nodded. "Good. You ever need anything from any of us, you have only to ask. All right?"

"Yes. I've got a lot of friends now. I never thought I'd ever have any." He looked around. "Aunt Sunny said that I had a reward coming, for helping with finding those little babies. You think it would be enough for a new bicycle? I don't want to ask Mom—Meghan said I could call her that—because she bought everything I could ever need. Kyle and Elliot, they got some nice ones, and I'd like to go riding with them sometimes. But don't tell Mom."

"No, I won't do that. I haven't any idea how much you'll receive." He said that he didn't really care, but thought it would be nice to have a bike. "I tell you what. You come out and shovel my driveway a couple of times, and I'll make up the difference for you. Deal?"

"Nah, I'd like to do that for you anyway. For today and saving my butt." Nathan leaned a little closer to him, and Adrian leaned in to him as well. So, in a whispered voice, Nathan asked him for a favor. "I'd like for you to teach me how to be an upstanding person. You know, like Great Grandda is always talking about what you are."

"It's a deal."

They shook on it, and then Nathan hugged him. Adrian had to stand with his back to everyone while he gathered up his emotions. Who knew that a hug could mean so much from someone that wasn't related to you by blood.

On his way home, Adrian called Henry. The two of them had been talking a great deal lately, mostly about football and food, but they were also talking about his life after being president. Henry had it in his head that he could retire and hide from the world for a time. Adrian thought he was nuts for even thinking that. The man was too well liked.

You are as well — you know that, don't you? He had to laugh at his brother, Evan when he poked into his thinking. *I have something to talk to you about with the hotel since Adam is so busy lately. Perhaps you could even join us on this venture? I'd love that. And I was thinking this should be a family thing anyway. So, I wanted your thoughts about having a few changes made to it before we start tearing things out. Grandda told me about this firm that he used to use when he needed work done. The man's name is Mason Jay Barnhart.*

Should I expect to have my mate turn up on this? They both laughed. *What sort of things do you have in mind? I'm on my way into town now. I had a few things to do, then I decided to get some dinner. Where are you?*

In the hotel. I came here with Dylan, but she was called away for some work. He told his brother he was sorry. *It's all right. It was making me crazy to be at home alone when she had to go out. But this project with you guys, it's giving me something to do.*

All right. Let me get some gas then I'll meet you there. I was thinking too that we should have Flora come by and see about the garden. I'm sure that she can tell us if it's worth saving or not. Some of the flowers and bushes are out of control. Evan said that he was thinking the same thing. *Great. I'll be there in about twenty minutes.*

Adrian wouldn't doubt that his brother had already contacted this Mason person for whatever project he had in mind, as well as had a quote on the job. Adrian knew that whatever it was that he wanted, it would be epic.

Chapter 11

Mas laid the phone in the cradle and leaned back on his seat. He wasn't sure that they'd have time to work with the Whitfield family, but he'd make sure that he had his best people on it if they got the job. Laughing when he heard his daughter in the hall, he wondered who had shit in her oatmeal. She was in a mood, it sounded like to him.

"I've had it up to my ass and beyond with that tile company we buy from. Did you know that they're charging us to bring the tile on site? I told him that if he decided to tack that onto his bill then we'd find.... What's the matter with you?"

Mas laughed. His little girl was a hoot, and she was smart as a whip and as mouthy as a rattler on a bad day. But she loved him and he her. She was the only thing in the world that would make him smile on even one of his worst days.

"You remember me talking about the Whitfields?" She asked if it was one of those rich fucks. "Yes—well, I don't think I'd group them in with the people we know. They're the good kind of rich. Mighty rich, I guess, but not like most think they are."

151

"Yeah? Well, I don't care so long as they don't try and buy us out."

That was a sore spot for the two of them. They'd grown their little company, mostly due to his daughter, up to where they could pick and choose who they wanted to work for. But now the bigger companies, the ones that they could outdo and outshine any day of the week, wanted to snatch them up and close them down. It broke his heart that his daughter had been so upset about it.

"I don't think they're in the business for a tile and paper company. But if they were, you can bet that their price would be more than fair, and if asked, they'd find all the people that worked for us other employment rather than put them out on the street." She asked him why he'd brought them up. "Oh, yes. The eldest of the boys, as Ollie, their grandfather calls them, is opening a hotel, revamping one with his brother. It's one of the kind that is too beautiful to want to plow down. He's sent me pictures—Evan, I believe his name is. The other one...I've forgotten his name, but this is what we'd be working with. Come have a look, honey. I think you might like to do this one all by yourself."

She came and stood behind him. Mas pulled up the file that had been sent to him yesterday. As she looked over the pictures, he read the specs on the place and what they would like to talk about. She had him pause on the one picture that he knew would capture her attention.

"That's the grand staircase. He said that the steps themselves are made of knotty pine, and the bracers on them are lined with brass. Also, the rails are a mixture of oak, cherry, and walnut. As you can see in this close up, they're blended together in no set pattern, but are beautiful because of that." Mason Jane Barnhart, his lovely daughter and partner, asked

152

him about the mural. "Not just a mural, it's stained glass. There are a few pieces missing. But Adam, that's his name, he said that there are plenty of leftover pieces that they've uncovered in the basement. Which, by the way, holds a large storage area and one of the biggest kitchen areas that he's ever seen."

"And it more than likely needs to be updated from walls to ceiling." Mas told her to behave. "Dad, this is some rich boy — man — that wants us to come in, do the work for less than half of what we'd usually charge, than stiff us for the rest."

"When did you become this hard, Mason? I've never known you to be so judgmental about people. Especially ones that you've never met." Her face blushed brightly, and she said that she was sorry. "I don't want you to be sorry. I want you to tell me what is going on."

She walked to the window in his office and stared down at the lot below them. Mas would have just as soon had the lower floor offices, but he'd been moved up here when he'd decided to retire. Mas didn't know whose idea that had been, but he hadn't moved back yet. "Angus is getting engaged, did you hear?" He said that he had and was happy for him. "Yeah, me too. He's a good person. After all he's been through, he deserves it. I told him that I'd throw him and Shelly a nice party when they were ready to announce it."

"You're not upset with your brother getting engaged. So, what is it that has you so snappy to others? I've not had any complaints, if you're thinking that. And you've been my daughter a lot longer than Angus has lived with us." He hadn't come to terms himself with the way that he'd ended up with Angus, nor would he ever forgive his mother. She had ruined a great many things with her lies. "What's happened to my little girl?"

"I'm far from a little girl, Dad. And no, I'm not upset about

153

Angus. You might say that I'm slightly jealous. Not a lot. I'm only just now realizing that I'm older than my brother, and I've not been on even a casual date since my senior prom." He asked her why she'd not. "I don't know. Perhaps I'm afraid. I think it's more than that, really, but I am afraid of dating."

"Mason, honey. What happened back then, it wasn't your fault." She nodded, and he could see the slight glistening on her cheek from tears. "Do you still hear from him? Does he still call you?"

"Once in a while. I've changed my number, and I don't think he's able to get it from anyone. He has tried the operator to reach me, but Andi no longer tells me when he does." Mas thought of Troy, the fucking bastard, and wondered if he could call someone to beat the shit out of him. "Dad, whatever you're thinking, let it go. He's not worth it."

But he was. Mas knew just what he'd done to Mason, and how badly he'd hurt her. It had been several years since that night, and since then his daughter hadn't been the same. She no longer seemed to smile, and she stayed at home, even when she'd been invited to someplace to celebrate a job well done. Mason did so few social events, people that they worked with thought her to be on her own. No, it was worth it to Mas. The man needed to be put in his place, once and for all. But he also knew that he'd made a binding promise to Mason to let it go.

"I'm going to let Angus take the lead on this project. I'll be there for him, but he can be the point man." Mas nodded. "If he gets married, then he'll need to be more involved in the business. He might be called in to take over for one or both of us."

"Are you going to leave me, child?" She turned to look at him, and Mas could see the pain on her face, almost touch how devastated she was. "Mason, tell me what's happened. What

154

did that bastard do to you?"

She didn't say anything. He worried more about her silence than he did her speaking to him. Again, she stood at the window. Mas could tell what she was looking at. It was just after five, and the staff would be leaving for the day. Cars would begin to pull away, the cleaning staff coming on. It was like this every day at this time. When Mason turned toward him she was no longer hiding her tears but letting the tears that were flowing show just how hurt she was.

"I'm going to take some time off when Angus is ready to be on his own. He's nearly there now, but he still has a few things to learn. I've been thinking about this for a while, Dad, so please don't talk me out of it." Mas told her that he'd not do that, so long as she promised not to simply leave for good. "I don't think that I have any more left in me, Dad. Maybe this will be all that I need. A place alone. But I can't make you a promise like that. Not at this point, that is."

"I love you, Mason. With all my heart. I don't know what I'd do if you were to just leave me." She walked around the office then, not touching anything there, which was her usual way of getting to the point. "Mason? Tell me what is it that has you so upset."

"I don't honestly know." She looked so lost that he wanted to pick her up and rock her as he'd done when she'd been very small. "I just need to get away I think. To get my head on straight. I think—no, I know that if I don't get away now, then I'll never feel right. Like a woman should at this stage in her life."

"I think I understand." She smiled at him, a watery one that made him so sad that he felt his own tears fill his eyes, his heart crumble a little more for her pain. "You'll help Angus with this project, right? Then we'll talk again. I just ask that you promise

155

to talk to me, to come to me before you just take off. Please?"

"I promise you." It was the best that he was going to get from her. When she was ready, she might tell him what was going on. Or, and this pained him more than anything, she'd just keep pushing him away in favor of not burdening him. Mas stood up when she made her way to his door. "If you want, you can tell the Whitfields that we'll work on their project. After, of course, we have a look. And I'll talk to Angus and let him know what to expect. All right?"

"Yes, of course."

With a nod, Mason, his lovely daughter, left him there. Mas knew that he had to make a few phone calls, but for the moment they could wait. He pondered what he really needed to do to help his only child, and what had brought on this sudden need to run away. Because as surely as he was sitting there, he knew that was what she was doing.

Just after finding out that Jane was with child, he'd been hit with a paternity suit. Mas not only didn't father Angus, but he'd not even known the woman he'd supposedly fathered Angus with. Almost as soon as Mabel Clark, the homewrecker, had put it in the paper that he'd abandoned her when she'd discovered that she was with child, his own wife had filed for divorce.

Not that hadn't expected this to happen. Jane had been unhappy since she'd found out that she was going to have a child. Mas had found out soon enough that he could strike a bargain with her, and she had lived up to her side of the bargain through it all. Jane would have the child, turning her over to him for full custody, and he'd pay her ten grand—a paltry amount, he thought—so that she'd leave them alone.

As it turned out, he'd not had to pay anything, not that he wouldn't have. The car accident that killed Jane had been just days after Mas had been sued, thus causing Mason to be brought into the world and his life just after her mother's death.

Months after that, Angus was dropped off at the police station, a note telling the officers there that she had no use for him and wanted his father, Mas, to have him. After that, Mas had considered his life to be complete.

He'd been so wrong. Not only had Mabel tried her best to get money from him, but she'd kidnapped Angus twice and once took Mason, each time abusing the children until he had to take matters into his own hands and pay her a ransom so that Mas could keep both his children safe.

She'd been in jail for a good month before he'd been able to get things straight with her. And to this day, it wasn't working out. She would pop back into their lives a few times a year, make a stink, then disappear until she needed money again. This last time, nearly twenty-four years after the children had been left in his care, Mas had sicced his daughter on her. That had worked better than he could have imagined. Smiling, Mas set to work on the new job.

The phone ringing had him pull his head out of what he'd been doing. Picking it up, not at all caring at this point who could be calling him, he said his name as he put in the last of his entries on another job that he'd been working on. When there was no answer at the other end, he said his name again.

"Mr. Barnhart, this is Doctor Evan Whitfield. I was calling you to ask if you've had time to go over the plans that we sent you." It took his befuddled mind a few seconds to remember who the man was. "I have gotten a call from someone in your offices, Angus Barnhart, to ask more questions as well. I wondered if that meant you were going to take us on."

"Yes. Oh, I'm so sorry. I was working on the next project, and I sort of — I'm sure you don't care what I'm up to. But yes,

Mason and Angus are my children, and they'll be working on this together. I'm to understand that Mason will be working with Angus to make sure that it will suit your needs. They are perfectly suited to each other. I would imagine that he'll call you several times until he can work you up a project and start there. Is that all right?"

"Perfectly. Thank you. I'll be looking forward to hearing from your boys." Mas started to tell him that they were one of each, his children, when the man spoke again. "I'm not on duty for the next few days after this one. My sister-in-law said that she'd cover for me when they can work us in. We're all— I have to go, sir. I'm on duty today."

The line went dead just as he heard in the background someone calling Dr. Whitfield's name. Hanging up, he smiled. They were going to be in for a rude awakening when Mason showed up. Yes, sir. This might be just the ticket to get her out of this funk. Mas might even go along with Angus to see the reaction on the faces of the men who had hired them. And be there when she lost her temper over someone thinking of Mason as being a man, not his daughter.

~*~

Adrian was going to have fun with the project that he'd been asked to work on. There were any number of places that a large factory could be put around the state. The list that he'd had emailed to him from different counties had been not only helpful, but also very detailed on the number of people that could be hired, men and women that were looking for work. He'd been given a list of companies—construction companies— that would gladly take on the construction that would be involved.

"You have a minute?" He looked up at his dad and grandda. "I don't suppose you could take a couple of old men out to

158

dinner, could you?"

Adrian glanced at the clock on his computer and realized that he'd been working through not just lunch, but dinner too. It was nearly six-thirty. Adrian wondered if Lily, his longtime secretary, had called them in to get him out of the building. He wouldn't put it past her.

"I don't mind having dinner with the two of you. But as far as old men wanting to join us, I'd rather just hang out with the two of you." Grandda laughed and Dad winked at him. "I've been working on some projects that I think I'd like your help with."

He explained what was going on and some of the feedback that he'd gotten from other counties around the area. Adrian told them about the businesses, two local ones, that wanted to expand, and three more that wanted to not only bring business to the area, but also put their home base here.

"Sounds to me like you're doing a bang-up job with this being governor and all. I cannot wait to tell your grandma about it when I see her." Adrian asked him not to say that. "You're right, I should have picked my words better. I'm going to tell her about this when I visit her where she's resting. I'm guessing that she's gonna need it once I join her in a few years. I'm happy now. With all you boys growing up and having mates — well, I have to tell you, it's the best pleasure that a man like me could have hoped for."

"Thanks, Grandda. You have no idea how much you saying that has done for me. I love you both, so very much."

They ended up just down the road from his place of business. Only just remembering that he'd given Lily the afternoon off, he remembered to lock up and shut off all the lights, with the help of his dad. He knew were they all were, while Adrian only had a vague idea.

The place wasn't all that busy, but everyone greeted his dad and grandda right away. He was proud of that, the fact that his grandda had taken a job working here, and that he'd taken so much pride in his work. The man could have bought and sold a hundred places like this one, even had a bigger crew working, without a dent in his money. That too was something that Adrian was happy for. His family supported everyone and everything.

They talked about the projects going on—not just what he had going, but his brothers as well. Not only were they involved in things, but his mom had been organizing a fundraiser for a few things and had the women helping too. Even if reluctant they were giving it their best.

"These here businesses that you're talking to—is one of them Mason Tile and Paper? I know him, or at least I know of him. He's about outgrown his little shop that he's got, and I'm afraid that should he get much bigger, someone is going to try and buy him out—and he just might let them." Adrian asked him why he thought that. "They'd be able to push him into a corner. You know, buy up every bit of property around him. Then when he wants to expand, there'll be no place for him to go. It would ruin a good man and his business. And his sons— I've only just found out that he has two of them. They work for their daddy full time."

Adrian was saddened by hearing that. He loved working for his dad when he was needed. And the fact that it was a family job made it all the more exciting to see it to completion each year when they brought in the crops. He'd have to look into this company and see if they'd be willing for him to do an analysis of the company and see what he could do for them. Adrian wasn't going to let a business fail when he could help them out.

They talked about this and that. Dad said that he'd see what he could discover about each of the plants that wanted to bring jobs to their area. Even though he'd already asked his sisters-in-law to do the same, the information that his dad would get him would be more on a personal level, and not so much the search and destroy kind of information. Dylan still didn't trust many people, and in a search, she would look for the darkest part of the company. Not looking at what they did for the people they worked for.

Walking home after dinner, he pulled his coat up around the collar and smiled at the snow coming down. The day after tomorrow was Thanksgiving, and he'd never been this excited about the holiday. There would be a crowd of people there — they'd invited some of the pack, as well as the police that weren't on duty. Some of the ones working had promised that they'd come by after their shift to grab a bite.

His house was almost finished too. He'd been thrilled to get such a good deal on the place. People were working on it, putting in security cameras, surveillance protection, as well as making his office a place that he could go to and know that he was secure. There had also been a safe room put in. They were finding that the electrical circuits weren't up to par, as well as the safe room would more than likely kill him and whoever was with him because of the shitty construction of the walls.

Just yesterday he'd been told that he needed all new outlets in the kitchen, as well as his office. Making sure that they weren't just padding his bill, Adrian went to see Sunny. Right away she was able to find out that they were not padding the bill, but they had been doing work for him that they'd not charged him for. He took care of that immediately.

There was a note on his door when he got home. Not touching it, he told Sunny what he'd found. The woman had an uncanny ability to touch something then be able to tell you not only who had done whatever it had been, but also anyone that worked with this person. She could see what their agenda had been. This time was no different.

Just touch the very tip of the paper. I should be able to get a great deal from that. He asked her if he should be worried. *Always. And I'm not kidding either. Now that you've put it out there that you wish to fill the presidency seat when it comes open, there will be a good many crackpots out to push you out of their way.*

Not so sure that she wasn't wrong about that, with trembling fingers he put his fingertip to the smallest part of the note as he could. When she laughed, he let out a long breath. Whatever it had been, there wasn't anything that had frightened her.

It's from your brother. Adam wants to know if you'd like to help him out with Thanksgiving. He thinks you make the best homemade rolls in the country. She laughed harder, and he felt his embarrassment go through the roof. *Should I tell him that you only call them homemade because you bake them there? Or should I tell him that you've been using frozen unbaked dough and passing it off as your own? You are, I suppose, making it at home, which will qualify for them being homemade. And you do thaw it out and work it into rolls too. You are a sneaky bastard, aren't you? I won't tell on you if you tell me how you do it. I'd like to have David argue with Adam on who makes the best rolls. Your secret is safe with me so long as you share.*

Deal. He plucked the note off the door and read it. It said just what she'd told him it would. Putting the note into his pocket, he unlocked the door and went inside. *Speaking of rolls and dinner, I've just had mine with Dad and Grandda. They're going to help me on a couple of projects around the state.*

He told her what it was going to entail and for her to help them when asked. Adrian was sure that they'd get around to asking her and the others. There was a good possibility that they'd know more about the companies than he could find by just researching them on the Internet. But Grandda and Dad, they'd find the heart of the person. And that was what he wanted more than anything.

Going to the kitchen, he realized that he was still hungry. When talking to his family, any of them, he'd not eat as much as he should. Adrian was always taking notes on what was being said, as well as talking around his food. It had always been easier for him to skip eating as much as he could and focus on what he wanted — information.

Pulling out the cold pizza from last night, he sat at the counter and ate two pieces while thinking about what he was up to. Over his head, he'd told himself more than once lately, but he'd been assured that he was doing great.

While munching on his fourth piece, he pulled out the paperwork that he'd been given today. It was about four businesses that he had tagged for helping out the state. One of them he wanted to mark off just because the name, to him, sounded sketchy. John Smith? He'd have one of the girls look into that one for him. Then he pulled open his laptop and began to do research on the company that his grandda had mentioned.

It had very good reviews was the first thing that he noticed. Out of seven thousand plus reviews, they still carried a four point eight. That was better than the construction company working on his home, including the one that Henry had recommended.

Adrian found a large article about the family — no names were mentioned, of course. But it said that the owner had been accused of infidelity and had won that suit, just when there was the trouble with his wife being killed in an automobile accident. It had laid squarely in her lap. The more Adrian read, the more he liked this unknown man. By midnight, Adrian had found nothing on the man that would have him think that they'd not work well together.

He had two sons, the article had claimed. Mason was one and Angus was the other. There were no pictures of any of the family, not even one of the wife when she'd been killed. But there was plenty to say on that matter. Nothing against Mas, as he liked to be called, but plenty on the accusations of a woman named Mabel Clark.

The woman had accused him of fathering her child. This was a trick that he'd seen used recently, on Meghan's young son, blaming Adam for fathering the child. Of course, this turned out to be for extortion, as it was impossible for Adam to father any child that didn't come from his mate, Ivy.

Smiling after putting all the paperwork away, Adrian sat down on the couch to watch the football game that he'd recorded. He should just go to bed, he knew that, but he had to let his mind settle. And football was the best way to do that.

Tomorrow was another day, a long work day, and he had enough on his plate and calendar right now that he'd be busy for the next fifty years. But he had to admit it, he was having a great time. And he thought that he'd make a good president as well.

Chapter 12

Adam wandered around the hotel again. He wasn't sure how much more he and Evan could do without professional help. Grinning, he thought of what sort of *professional* help they might really need. Coming down the staircase, as always he could see it finished, people coming in and out of the place. That was when he knew they could do this.

"Hello." The man standing in the front lobby smiled at him. "I'm Angus Barnhart. I was told that I could meet Mr. Whitfield here. Or a Doctor Whitfield. I'm with Mason Tile and Paper."

"Oh yes. I forgot that you were coming today. My brother is working—on call—but I can help you with whatever you might need for today." The younger man nodded and looked around. "Do you think that you can help us out?"

"Oh yes. We've been in business for a long time, and we specialize in older places, redoing the walls and floors to match the time they were built in. This is from the late eighteen hundreds, I believe." Adam was impressed. He'd gotten the time right, and his positive attitude had him believing that they had a good chance of making this work. When Angus walked over to the front desk, something that Adam thought had to go, Angus pulled out a small crowbar and lifted a square of tile off the top. "Just as I thought. You can keep this or not, but we can bring this wood up to its original beauty, and I'm betting that since this is wood, you'll find that the sides are also the same work."

He flushed brightly, and Adam smiled. "I think we might be able to work well together."

"I'm sorry for not asking first if I could tear up your counter this way. My dad said that I need to work on this." Angus laughed, but his face was no less red. "I get excited on projects such as this one. Most people would have gutted the place and made it all plush and modern. I prefer the old over the new. The antiquated aspects of a place that make us remember, while not the best of times, that there were other times than where we are now."

"I'll have to take you to my brother's house. He had everything about it redone to match the time period. With a few alterations for better plumbing and such." Angus told him that he'd enjoy that. "Good. And if your firm is anything like you, I'd count on having the job."

"Thank you. I only need to take some video of the entire place, one room at a time. If you don't mind." Adam told him that he could do whatever he wanted. "Are you thinking from top to bottom or just an overhaul of this area, Mr. Whitfield?"

"Call me Adam, please, and the entire place. With the exception of a couple of the rooms being turned into suites, we're going to bring it up to code. We also want to add Wi-Fi and convenience things such as that but have them blend into the rest of the place. Can that be done?"

Angus was looking around the main floor. Adam followed him because he was liking the way the man seemed to be searching for any flaw in the place, things that others who had owned the hotel had done to bring it up to whatever design they had in mind for it.

Twice more he pulled something away from the wall. Once he peeled back carpet to show hardwood floors—not just hardwood, but a floor that had been made into a design, oaks and walnut in a pattern that circled the room. Adam knew that neither he nor Evan had thought of what might have been under the carpets, and wondered if there were more little treasures like these. And Angus took pictures of everything that he did.

After getting a call from his dad, Adam told Angus how to get in touch with him. The huge tablet sort of thing was turned on now, and he was going around each room describing what he was seeing and what he'd discovered. Adam watched him for a few minutes more before leaving him to his work. Excited as all hell, he talked to his brother on the way to his parents' home.

"You remember your Aunt Bea, Grandda's sister, Bea Whitfield?" He told his dad that he did and shivered. "Yeah, right there with you, son. She's coming for a visit. I was thinking that maybe you can find her a house to rent—one on the other side of town so she's out of our hair. Dad has a couple, but he said he's not having her that close to us. I can't blame him on that. She's a bit of a nosy biddy, and—well, a lot of other things too. But if you could find her something, like I was saying, it'd be much appreciated, son."

"How long will she be here?" Dad said too long, but Mom told him that it was to be until after the holidays. "In which year? I mean, the last time she stayed through the holidays, I think she was here for four or five years."

"Yes, well, we'll cross that bridge when we have no choice." Adam had to hide a smile. Aunt Bea had never married, as far

167

as he knew, but she wasn't shy about telling anyone how many lovers she'd had between this time and the last time you might have seen her. "She said that she only wants four bedrooms. I don't know how old she thinks you boys are, but she wants room for you to be able to spend the night."

"I'm thinking that none of us will take her up on that. I think that we're all a little too old for sleepovers. In fact, I don't think any of us spent the night with her at any time." Dad shivered this time. "Dad, she can't be as bad as she used to be, can she? I mean, she has to be in her eighties, right?"

"Ninety-four. And she's not changed a lick." Dad sat down and looked at him with pleading on his face. "I know that Josh usually does this sort of thing—you know, finding housing and such. But he's helping Adrian with a speech that he has to give at the White House in a few days. Aunt Bea is coming to invade us on Thursday morning. Told us to hold Thanksgiving for her. Like she rules the roost."

"Oh, stop being so dramatic, Oliver. You know as well as I do that she's not that bad. Just too opinionated and loud about it." Mom smiled when she looked at Adam. "She's going to be so happy that you boys are having mates and children. We have so many now, and more on the way with Sunny due at the first of the year. I'm thinking that the news of children will mellow Bea out some. At least that's what I keep telling myself."

Adam asked Josh what he had on the books for a rental, long term. After getting a list from Dad's office in the form of an email, he took it home with him. There weren't that many on the market for rentals. There were a great many smaller homes, homes that the bank had seized, as well as a couple more that had to be torn down because of the terrible shape they were in. As soon as Ivy came home, he told her about his aunt.

"She sounds like she'd fit right in with this family." He

thought about what she said and realized that she was right. Aunt Bea might be rendered speechless when she met up with the Whitfield women of this family. Ivy looked over the list, as well as the one for the things Aunt Bea wanted in a house. "From this list, I'd say your aunt is lonely. Who wants a large house like this one when they're only renting? Someone hoping for a visit now and then. Also, she wants live-in help, a cook, as well as someone to take care of the yard. There isn't any reason for her to have her yard attended to if she's only here through the holidays. It's winter, no need for her trees to be pruned or her flowers planted. I can see that she might like a cook. But a staff of ten? Nope, this is a person that needs company."

He looked over the list again with fresh eyes. There were other things on the list that Adam noticed. She wanted a driver. Yes, that he could see as well. When she'd been younger, she'd been hell on wheels, as Grandda told him. And them being sister and brother, he'd know best.

Without looking up from the list, Adam reached out to confirm with his parents when she was to arrive. When they said Grandda was on his way to talk to him, Adam knew something was up, especially after he saw the look on his face.

"She's here isn't she?" Grandda answered him with a grumble. "When did she get here? I'm assuming recently, correct?"

"This morning. She came in, made sure we were working on that blasted list, and left, to stay, temporarily she told me, at the local B&B. Do you think we could hire someone to take her out and leave her there?" He looked at his grandda. Adam was sure that he'd ever heard him say something like that before. "Well, you can't blame me. She went to your mom's house with white gloves on and swiped them all over the place. She didn't find anything, of course. But you have no idea how nervous it makes us when she does something like that."

"Mom runs a tight ship, Grandda. And I'll save you if she comes around here pushing her way around." He had no idea how he was going to stop that. Aunt Bea scared the crap out of all of them, except for Blake. For some reason, probably because he was the youngest, he could get away with more than the rest of them. "I think, I hope anyway, that she'll be easier to be around once she sees the children and the mates. And you know as well as I do that none of them will take any crap from her."

Grandda smiled. It was bright enough that Adam was sure that he could see by it in the darkest of nights. In that moment, Adam was sure that he'd do anything in the world for the man. Not that he wouldn't have before, but he made him feel all powerful.

Adam hung around his house until dinner. Everyone was going to the house to meet the *old bag*, as Grandda called her. None of the rest of them could do that. No one that he knew would ever say anything like that to Aunt Bea's face. But he was also glad to know that she'd be meeting his own mate.

As smells began to permeate the rooms as soon as he was in his parents' house again, he felt his mouth water. He knew that tomorrow afternoon, Thanksgiving Day, at his house would have a smell explosion. Every veggie, plus the turkey and ham, would be cooking. There would be roast pork and homemade breads. And gravy. Christ, he was full just thinking about what dinner would bring.

Adam had taken the list of foods that he could remember them having every year and passed it onto Nate. And even though he'd never spent a single holiday with them as yet, Nate was just as excited as he was. Then there would be Christmas.

His family would go all out on those two holidays. All of

them really, but the big ones were the last two holidays of the year. Not even his birthday could compare to the food that would be made, the groans that could be heard during the entire day. Then there was football.

They didn't really have a team that they only rooted for, not like some people did. The Whitfields just enjoyed football. Other sports too, but nothing like the leather ball that was kicked up and down a beautiful field to score.

Adam knew the moment that his aunt was in the house, and met his only true love, Ivy.

"This young woman, she said that she belongs to you, Adam." Ivy told her that she'd said no such thing, and that she never belonged to anyone. "Whatever makes you rest easily. Is this true?"

"Yes. She is my mate. The rest of it, you're on your own with that one, Aunt Bea. I would like to point out that she does have a mind of her own." Aunt Bea snorted. "She's working with Evan."

"A nurse?" Ivy told her that she was a renowned surgeon and worked all over the world. "Yes, well, don't you think that you'd be better off staying at home, being a good wife and cooking my nephew a nice dinner?"

"No, I don't think that at all. If he wants a milksop of a woman, one who'll wait on him hand and foot, then he'd better be making out his will and buying himself a nice plot. I don't put up with the thought that women are too stupid to breathe without a man around." Aunt Bea looked as if she had more to say on the subject, but Ivy cut her off. "I'm a good wife to him. Him a better husband than I could have ever asked for. I cook when I please, which isn't all that often. I don't make the bed. I would, I suppose, if I was the last one in it, but usually I'm in the hospital before the sun comes up."

"Are you saying that you're better than my nephew because you get to cut people open?" Ivy crossed her arms over her chest and stared at his aunt. "Intimidation doesn't work with me, young lady. I've been around for a very long time, and I know tricks that you'll never understand."

"Do you now? And for the record, you started this bullshit. I haven't any idea if this is the way you treat everyone, but you won't be walking all over me. Not today, not ever. You might want to stick that feather in your cap too." When Grandda snickered, Aunt Bea turned her eyes on him. "You hurt him either, by word or deed, and I'll show you tricks that will turn you inside out and backwards so quickly that you'll think it was all a bad dream. Watch yourself, old lady, or I swear to Christ and all that is holy that you'll rue the day you ever opened that flapping mouth of yours."

No one moved. Adam was reasonably sure that no one was breathing either. While he didn't much care for his aunt's words most of the time, Ivy had just threatened her with bodily harm. When Aunt Bea turned and looked at him, Adam felt his tongue stick to the roof of his mouth, his legs weakening at the thought of what she might say to him next.

When she pointed her boney finger into his chest, hard and repeatedly, he started to tell her that he was sorry about Ivy and that he would.... Well, he wasn't sure what he'd do. Not tell her she was wrong, because it had been Aunt Bea who had started it.

"You keep this girl, Adam. She knows up from down and won't steer you wrong if you need someone in your corner. And if you need someone to kick your ass into something, I'm betting all I own she'll do it and not care one bit if you lose it all. You hear me?" Adam told her that he loved Ivy. "We'll, you'd be a damned fool if you didn't."

Aunt Bea stood in front of Ivy who looked as relaxed as she did every day. Only a few knew the turmoil that was going through her mind at any given moment. The only time that he'd known her not to stress was when she was in the operating room and doing what she did best.

"You, my dear, are going to go far. Not too far. I don't want anything to go to your head. And don't think I didn't know about you before coming here. I have a good head on my shoulders, and I know how to use a computer. And what I didn't find out there, I found out where I wanted. You are a great surgeon. Now, give me a hug. I think I deserve one after the tongue lashing I got, don't you?"

"I do. But this wasn't a game of power, Ms. Whitfield. You really will be sorry if you hurt anyone in my family. I know that you are family as well, but you won't be long if you fuck with me." Aunt Bea laughed. It was hardy and full of mirth. And when the two of them hugged, Adam could see that it was robust as well. "I think I might like you, Ms. Whitfield."

"Call me Bea. I don't allow that much familiarity when I just meet people, but I like you. A great deal." She looked around the great hall where the rest of them were standing and pointed out the women. "Come on now, let's get to know each other. I tell you, I might just have to stick around, teach some of you manners before all is said and done. Yes, ma'am, this might be just the place I lay down my hat."

When they entered the living room, Dad came over and hugged him. When he asked him what that was for, he laughed.

"I should have done that years ago. I might well have slept better before and while she was visiting." He laughed again. "Of course, she might have hit me through the wall or something had I done it. Yes, your mate? She's the ticket. Cannot wait to meet the rest of the brides coming here. It's going to be a fun time for all, I believe."

Adam joined them all in the living room. Blake stopped him and looked like he might be sick. Adam asked his brother what was wrong, and he looked into the living room before answering.

"I'm not going to survive a mate if she's anything like yours. Any of them, as a matter of fact. I'm so fucked." Adam laughed. "You think this is funny now — wait until one of them takes you to task for something. You won't then." Adam wondered what had happened and decided that he didn't care. He was home, mated, and happy. That was all right in his book.

~*~

Ivy had no idea what had come over her to talk to an elder like she had. Of course, it had turned out all right, but still, that wasn't like her to do something so rude. When Adam sat on the arm of the couch she was sitting on, he kissed her head and took her hand into his.

I was so rude. Not that I really think I shouldn't have been, but I don't talk to people that way. He told her that his aunt brought out the worst in everyone. Then he told her what his dad had said. *Well, he's not wrong on that. But I just don't know what the hell came over me.*

Her. Listen love, even her brother was dreading her coming over tonight. They only see each other once or twice a year. I don't have any idea why she might even be here now. But I have to say, I was terrified that she was going to pull out a gun and pop you in the head with it. Ivy asked if he was kidding. *Yes. She'd never use it on your head. I think she'd use it elsewhere, a larger area to hit. But if you're asking if she carries, yes, she does. Has for years.*

That didn't make her feel any better. But now that the tension seemed to have dissipated, she was getting on better with everyone. Ivy had a feeling that the woman was here under false pretenses. There was another motive for her being here at this time. Something terrible, and Ivy was afraid it was serious.

Dinner was called about thirty minutes later. It was hard to equate this thing with a dinner—it was a huge feast. There were platters of food on the table. Sideboards were opened up to full capacity, and there was more food there—cakes and pies as well as cookies as big as her hand. When Nathan came to her, asking what to do, she told him that he'd better fill his plate, because she was hungry enough to eat it all. Laughing, he filled up two plates of food and went to the table that held his new cousins.

Meghan looked just as lost. Ivy bumped her with her hip as she waited for her turn at the platters. "I thought for sure that woman was going to bite your head off. Shift, you know, and take you down." Ivy told her sister that she was a bigger cat and she was younger. "That's not funny. I was worried you'd gone too far."

"So was I, if you want to know the truth." Meghan laid her head on her shoulder. "Are you all right, sis? I mean, is motherhood taking its toll on you? I can watch Nathan if you need some time. I know that I'd have to have an adjustment period getting used to kids."

"You would not. You'd be right in there in the thick of things. No, I'm all right with Nathan. We're having a good time with the house. I just hope we don't do something terrible with it so that Ollie kicks us to the curb." Ivy didn't say anything to her, but she knew that Ollie was going to gift it to Meghan for a Christmas gift. "I've found myself a job. I wasn't going to be able to sit around the house, just waiting for Nathan to come home. Your mother-in-law, she invited me to come and help her at the historical society. It's fun. My college courses are finally going to pay off."

They were both laughing as they filled their plates. The table in the dining room was stretched out into the secondary room which Ivy had often wondered what the space could be used for, and today she had her answer. The doors had been slid into the pockets on the wall, and the table, already a mammoth of a thing, had been pulled apart and eight more large leaves were put in. Christ, the table had to be at least ten feet long when in regular usage. Now it was nearly twenty feet long, and seven or so feet wide. It was a table meant for a large family. She asked Eve where she hid all the chairs and leaves when not in use.

"Oh, my. You'd have to talk to Adrian about it. When he was in high school and college, he tinkered, as he called it, in making large things take up the least amount of space. This table, it was his graduation project. Believe it or not, there are four more leaves where these were. Under the wider slats are braces that hold the leaves when not in use." She showed it to her by lifting up the table cloth. "The chairs all hang on the walls in the basement. They're all wrapped up in burlap bags that have been treated to keep bugs and such away. Being cats, we don't have a lot of trouble with rodents."

"I would guess not." They were both laughing when Adam sat down beside her and kissed her on the forehead. "Are all cats like you? All cuddly and stuff."

Yesterday Ivy had had a long talk with one of the nurses at the hospital. She told her all kinds to things that she'd not known about shifters and straightened out some things that she'd been told that were not necessarily a lie, but they weren't quite the truth either.

"You think I'm cuddly? I think you are too." He smiled at her as he touched her mind. *I'd like to take you home right now and show you just how cuddly I can be. It's been a long time since I've had you beneath me. Or for that matter, just naked. I love it when you're naked. Makes me hard as stone.*

Behave yourself. We're at your parents' home. Adam wiggled his brows at her and she laughed. No one asked her what was so funny, nor did they tease her. She supposed that when everyone could talk to each other like her and Adam were, there was no reason to have to explain anything. *I'm going to make you so hard then walk away from you. Just for teasing me like this.*

Adam took her hand and slid it over the length of his cock. He was already stone hard, and she wanted to get up and find them a dark corner. The only problem that she could see was that she'd have to be quiet when she came. Ivy was a screamer since she'd met this man and didn't want to hold back when he took her. And when he leaned over and nipped at her earlobe, hard enough to make her hurt, she couldn't have stopped the moan if she'd had tape over her mouth.

Again, no one seemed to notice. And when she told Adam to behave once again, he complied. If they kept playing around at the table, they were going to hurt each other. Eating no longer held an appeal for her, but she knew that she'd need her strength for later. Yes, she told herself, she was going to make him pay for this.

Chapter 13

As soon as they were in the door to their own home, Ivy expected Adam to rip her clothing off, move her to the floor, and take her hard. But he only touched her, running his fingers over the back of her neck to her shoulders, then up and down the bare part of her arm. When she moaned he smiled at her, but it had the look of a predator, like he was not only going to devour her, but he was going to do it slowly.

"Have you changed your mind?" He told her that he'd not, but he had other things in the works for her. "Am I going to enjoy it?"

"Have I ever disappointed you before?" Adam wasn't the type of man to take what he needed and leave a woman hanging, and she told him this. "I need to check on what is going on in the kitchen. You should come too. Nate said that he had a couple of questions about the cake you wanted."

Her disappointment was profound. He wanted to check on the kitchen? She followed him but could hear her own footsteps as she pouted like a small child, stomping her feet as she moved across the floor. As soon as they were in the kitchen, Ivy could only stare at the wonderment that was there.

"This is...I don't have words to describe this. All this, it's for tomorrow?" He nodded, checking the notes that had been left for him. At one point he frowned, so Ivy walked to where he was. "What's wrong?"

"I ordered some things for dinner that won't be here tomorrow. It was for the kids. I'm sure that they like this sort of thing, especially the way they chowed down on it tonight. But I had asked for some burgers to be made up, in the event they weren't into more ham. I suppose they could have turkey."

"Adam, I think if they didn't like ham, there are enough other items here that they could eat." Looking around, she pulled a carrot stick from the platter. "I'm so full, but these look so good I can't help myself. Is there anything else that we need to fix tonight? I'm bushed."

He said that he'd lock up and she made her way up the stairs. It was reasonable to think that he'd be exhausted. The two of them had been up since dawn, her just a little longer. And hanging out with family, no matter how nice they were, could be exhausting.

Ivy put her phone on the charger, then decided to turn it off in favor of getting a good night's sleep. She wasn't on call, and she and Evan both had the next three days off. With the influx of people coming into town, so had their need for more physicians. They'd interviewed seven so far and hired three of them. She was thrilled for the extra hands on call.

She was just slipping into the bed when Adam came into the room and sat on the side of the bed. She waited to see what was on his mind when he moved toward her—stalked would have been a better word—but she was suddenly so tired that she couldn't make her befuddled mind work the words out.

"Stand up and I'll give you a massage." Ivy started to turn

him down when he pulled his shirt up and over his head. "I promise that I'll make it worth your while."

Standing up, she pulled her hair around so that it hung over her right shoulder. Ivy didn't hear him move, but his hands touching the tense muscles at her neck had her moaning loudly. All he'd done was touch her, just run his fingers over the tense muscles over her neck to her shoulder, and she felt revived. Reaching to the wall, she planted her hands there so as to hold on to something before he killed her.

His fingers dug deeply into her worn and tired muscles. It hurt on occasion, but it made up for any amount of pain when he'd kiss the hurt away. Everywhere his fingers touched her, every time his fingers soothed over her skin, Ivy would moan. Stopping it, or even trying to stop it, would have been nearly impossible.

"Your skin, it tastes like lemon drops, bright with color. I can almost bite into your flesh to taste all of you." Again she moaned, and her knees were getting weaker. "I've never thought of a color as being tasty, but I swear to you, Ivy, it's as if I can see the color with my eyes closed while I nibble on your skin."

He did just that, pulling the small straps of her nightgown down her arm as he nipped none too gently at her flesh. Ivy would have sworn that he was marking her, his mouth doing things to her skin that no one else would be able to see. Leaning her more against the wall that was in front of her, Adam pressed his cock into the bottom of her ass.

She wasn't just wet but soaking, and the fine dewy sweat had the hairs on her skin dancing, the flesh below it coming alive. The more that he touched, everywhere that he would mark her, Ivy knew that her skin would never be the same. Nor would her heart. And when he bit down on her shoulder, where her neck connected with her head, Ivy had a hard, dangerously strong climax that took her breath away. Her heart even stopped beating for several seconds.

"Turn around, love." She told him that she'd fall. "Good. Because while you're on the floor, I can make love to you."

Ivy fell to the floor. Had he not been there when she let go of the wall, she was sure that both of them would have been injured. As he was helping her to the floor, she realized that she was naked and so was he. Her body was on fire, her skin as sensitive as she'd ever felt it be. And when he sat on her, his legs on either side of her, Ivy reached up to touch him as he had her, but he pushed her hands back to the floor.

"I've been thinking all day about this. Touching you and making you mine." Ivy told him that she belonged to him and no other. "And I belong to no one but you. Forever and a day, I'll belong to you heart and soul."

He could spin a web of words that would make her feel secure, make her believe that not only was it raining and she stood in the sunshine, but that he could love her in ways, not just with his hands and body, that she would cherish forever. When his hand moved over her, this time over her breasts and face, Ivy cried out, louder each time, with her release and enjoyment, so that he'd know just what he was doing to her.

Her body was limp. She'd come so many times that she had nothing more to give. Ivy was sure that if she came one more time, just once more, she'd be nothing more than a puddle of flesh. But Christ, she'd go willingly to feel like this forever.

"I need you." Telling him no was impossible. "I want to feel you wrapped around me. Your sheath holding me tightly within you so that when you come with me, I'll feel each muscle, every ripple of your body."

"I'm done." He laughed and told her that she was far from

finished. "No, you don't understand, I'm done coming. I'm having a hard enough time just remembering to g—"

Adam slid deep inside of her. There was no pain, just his heat taking her to another level, surpassing anything that she'd ever felt before. And when he moved, his body fully touching her own, Ivy screamed out his name at the top of her lungs when he bit down hard on her shoulder—marking her, she knew, so that anyone, any male or cat would know that she'd been claimed.

The lick across the wound gave her a surge of energy. She wrapped her legs around his hips, giving him anything he wanted so that he'd plow her deeper, harder. When Adam threw back his head, his cat racing over his face and chest, Ivy watched in deep satisfaction as he filled her body with the hottest part of them, the part of him that she would treasure forever.

Adam dropped atop her. She didn't care that he was heavier than her, didn't mind that he'd bumped her head when he fell. They were connected still, in the most intimate way possible. The way a loving couple did when they could never forget how much they loved their partner.

Waking up, still on the floor, Ivy looked at Adam as he slept quietly. His arm was over his eyes and his body was spread out like he was king of the castle. He was to her—he was also the owner of her heart.

Getting up, putting one of the larger throw blankets over him, Ivy went to take a shower. It was nearly seven anyway, and she needed a good run. The land around the house had been cleaned around, and any dangers, such as fallen trees or branches, had been removed just for her.

Ivy made her way to the kitchen. She'd nearly forgotten the bustle of today. There were several people that she didn't know, but Nate still had time to make her something to eat. Making her sit, he told her what was going on today.

"I've hired a lot of the high school kids to come by and help out. Ms. Eve had been doing this for years, and it helps some of the poorer families with the supplies, as well as the little extras that come about in the year." He asked her if she had any preferences.

"No, none. It'll be good that we can help out. They're not going to miss their own dinner, are they?" Nate smiled at her. "Yes, well, I might be selfish enough to want all the help we can get. But I don't want anyone missing a fantastic dinner like the feast we're having."

"You're no more selfish than Ms. Eve is, silly. They're each only working a few hours at a time. We've made it so that no one goes without. In addition to the money they're getting paid, they're each going to receive a turkey that can be baked at anytime they wish. Most of the adults working today are also going home with enough side dishes and pies that their meal isn't going to be any extra expense for them."

After eating her bagel and cream cheese, Ivy took off for the path, skipping over piles of snow and puddles of water. The fresh air with just a little bite of crispness in it was just what she needed today to blow out the cobwebs of the last few days.

She was still a little at odds with their Aunt Bea. The woman had startled her enough that she'd fought back verbally with her. Usually Ivy wasn't one to argue with someone like the elder Whitfield, but she had brought out some kind of defensive mood that had her wanting to hit her. Ivy had not ever had such a feeling before.

Then last night, just as they were all leaving, she heard her talking on the phone. Not one to eavesdrop on anyone, she paused in the middle of making her way to the bathroom to see what was going on.

"I think this is the right one." The person on the other end was easy for Ivy to hear, but she was not able to make out what they were saying. "Yes, yes, I'm aware of that as well. You will not take that tone with me, young man, or so help me, I'll expose you right now."

There was a shuffle, like someone sitting up straighter in a chair, then the conversation began again. It made her nervous, only hearing one side of the call, but she thought that she'd heard enough to surmise that whoever Ms. Bea was talking to, she didn't much care for them.

"I have done just what you wanted me to do, have I not?" The answer was clearer, the person on the other end of the call spoke loud enough for her not only to hear what they said, but also that it was a man. "Then you'll leave me alone? You'll take care of what you promised to do for me?"

The answer was a deep throated laugh, then the line went dead. To hide herself to think about it, Ivy stepped into the small bathroom and shut the door. Ivy flushed the toilet and washed her hands before coming out into the now empty hallway. But for the rest of the night, she kept a close eye on Bea.

Just as she was rounding the bend in the path to take it back to the house, a large cat stepped in front of her. She knew immediately who it was. Stopping and taking several steps back, her fear of the elderly cat had her reaching for anyone that could hear her.

Her shift from animal to woman was quick. On some level Ivy knew that she shouldn't be dressed, but she had more pressing things on her mind than clothing. Bea leaned over and picked up a gun—not pointing it at her, not yet, but it wouldn't take much effort to bring it up and kill her.

"I'm in trouble." Ivy nodded. "I know that you heard me

last night. I waited there for about an hour before I made the call that I wanted you to know about. I was hoping...well, to be honest with you, I'm not sure what I was hoping. But I'm in deep trouble."

"Are you going to use that? If so, you should know that I've spoken to Evan and Josh. They're both on their way." Bea nodded and looked around. Ivy, if it was a trick, didn't do the same. "What is it you think that I can help you with? Or for that matter, why would I want to do anything for you?"

"I had to do that, fight with you. I wanted to catch you off guard, show you that while I'm an old woman and cat, I can take on a much younger person than myself. But you didn't touch me. Had you done that, then I'd have had a connection with you." Ivy knew that as well. There had to be some kind of blood exchange. "I wanted you to kill me."

"I wouldn't have done that. Not unless you hurt one of the others."

Bea said that she could see that now.

Evan came through the woods first, his cat twice the size of Bea's when she'd come out of the woods. Josh was next, and with him was Adam.

"She said that she's in trouble. I don't know what's going on just yet."

"I'm being blackmailed. They've taken all that I had. Not just money, but—well, anything else that they thought I no longer needed." Evan must have said something to his aunt. When she looked at Ivy, she felt her sorrow and fear double for the other woman. "Evan said that he'd gladly help me. I knew that he'd say that, but I think that the only person that can help me is you, Ivy. And if you turn me down, I'm as good as dead right now."

~*~

Evan paced the long room. It was about three hours before anyone in the family would show up to eat, and he was sick with worry that something would go wrong. When Dylan came to him, he reached for her to hug, but instead he got a smart slap to the face.

"What the fuck was that for?" She told him he was projecting. "Yes, well, so are you, but you're a bit more violent with it. Really, what did you hit me for, love?"

"As I said, you're projecting. And anyone within ten feet of you can see that you're afraid. Stop it. Think of something else. Anything else." Evan told her that it was difficult. "Yes, I'm sure it is. But think of this—if you give this up, then a lot of people are going to be hurt, perhaps killed."

There was that. Just a little over an hour ago, he had sat down with his family. He had to admit, they were scary when they came together for a common cause. Now he was questioning a great many things that had happened over the last twenty-four hours, especially where his aunt was concerned.

Like her showing up right out of the blue. She'd have her *surprise* visits, but she'd always give them at least week before descending on them. Aunt Bea would like for people to be prepared for her when she arrived. He thought that was the only reason she came about five to seven days after announcing that she was on her way. That and the uproar that came with it.

But what she'd told them today, just this morning, Evan had to sit down and let it wrap around his mind before he traveled that well-worn path again. He looked up at his mom when she said his name.

"Dylan said that I should knock you around a bit. I don't want to, but it would go a long way in making me feel like I'm being productive." Evan smiled and took her hand into his larger one and kissed the back of his mom's. "She's never been in trouble before this. She's *been* trouble. Bea has always danced to her own set of cymbals."

Evan laughed, which he was sure that she'd intended him to do. Sitting down on the couch next to him, she leaned her head on his shoulder and sighed heavily. Evan watched the women in his family talk and plot.

"They're brilliant, aren't they?" He didn't ask her who she was talking about but nodded. "Apart they're a bigger force than I think that even an army would have. Together, I do believe that they could move a mountain or two. If any one of them were to start a war, I'd defect to a place that I'd find safer. Not that I think they'd harm me, but I think the fall out is going to be epic."

"You need to stay away from Dylan, Mom. You're beginning to sound just like her." She thanked him. "It wasn't a compliment. I was telling you that it's not a good thing—not for my mom, anyway—to sound like my wife. She's mouthy and full of spit and sausage, as Grandda says."

"Yes, well, there a great deal to be said about acting like someone you admire. And I do admire them. Every one of them." She laughed a little, and he had to smile. "Oh Evan, can you imagine what the next two mates are going to be like? My goodness, we'll have a houseful before long. And no one will come within fifty feet of this family if they know what's good for them."

"I agree." He watched as Sunny got up and then sat down again. Three times. "She's not happy with the plan, I take it."

"No, Sunny is upset that she didn't think if it first. Adam's mate, our lovely Ivy, is scary organized. Is she like that in the operating room?" Evan told her she was, and that Ivy listened to classical music, and everything was in place before she even picked up an instrument. "I figured as much. The two of you would never get along as well as you do if not. You've always been very organized. Even as a child."

The doorbell going off was the signal that they'd all been waiting for. While the plan had been hammered out and then relooked at several times over, calling the man to come to the house had been the only recourse that they had. Then the hard part came. They'd have to operate on his aunt.

He and his mom, under orders from the people hidden among his family members, had stayed out of sight. The only people that could be seen by the men were his aunt, Grandda, as well as Ivy. Rachel and Nathan were under lock and key in the kitchen, where they'd be safe. They'd not stand a chance if this went sour.

"Beautiful—how are you faring this fine day?" The man's voice was nasal, sounding like he'd been at a football game or something like that, and he'd screamed all night at the coach. Evan knew that feeling—he'd been to a great many— "We have an understanding, you and I. And I see that you've held up your end of the bargain quite well."

"You make it sound as if I had any kind of choice in the matter. Do whatever it is you want, and I'll be on my way to the grandchildren's house for dinner. Not that I'll be eating all that much. You've pretty much ruined my ever enjoying this holiday again. And it being my favorite." He told her to shut up. "I will do no such thing. What is it you want? Your pound of flesh? I'm sorry, but I've given all that I can today. You'll get no more from me."

The man laughed again before speaking. "You'll do just as you are told. Now, move out of my way so that I can take the good doctor here with me. A great many people are going to sing my praises once I show up with a surgeon to help our leader." Aunt Bea snorted at him. "You don't think my reasons are good enough for having blackmailed you into doing this? Well, not that I care what you think—I will be honored greatly for this."

"You really think that I'm going to go with you easily? If so, then you're fucking nuts." Ivy's voice was calm—hard but calm. "Why don't you fucking crawl back under the rock you slipped out from under and leave us alone?"

"I was told that you were full of your own self-worth." No one said anything, but Evan saw the moment when something happened. "You will come with me or I'll kill this lovely woman here. She's worth a great deal more to me dead than alive anyway. Perhaps I can kill her now, threaten you with the same thing, and take you anyway. There is no one here to gainsay me. You do know that you'll never get out of here alive."

"Really? Well, I hate to tell you this, but you're fucking wrong. And what sort of person would I be if I just left here with you without a single thought?" The room seemed to have come alive in that moment. There were so many people surrounding him and his mom that Evan couldn't see what was going on by the doorway. But when he heard Dylan laughing, Evan felt like the air had been let out of his head and he was relieved by it.

Aunt Bea was taken to the room to the left of the dining room. She had a small explosive planted in her leg that needed to be removed before some idiot on the other side of the world got wind of the capture of these men today and killed her. As soon as it was removed from deep within her leg, it was handed first to Sunny, then to the men that had come with Henry Cobb.

Sunny was able to find that there was two more in Aunt Bea's body. One was up near her neck, alongside her spine. The other was in her right hand, near her wrist, that he supposed was to take off her hand if she became too much trouble. Dylan told him that it was more than likely put there so that she'd bleed out slowly. It was what she might have done. It would have made her suffer once it had been fired off. He asked her never to tell him that sort of stuff again.

After they were all removed, he and Ivy sat down on the room's only two seats. It hadn't been that bad, the removal of the explosives, but it had been stressful. This was his aunt. While he wasn't sure that he liked her all that much, she was still blood, and they took care of all family members when they needed it.

"She saved my life." Evan had never thought of it that way but told her he was sorry. "Yes, well, I'll be beholden to her for the rest of my days, and I'm going to damn well make her feel grateful that I'm so nice to her. The old biddy had the nerve to tell me that I'm too young to be motherless. I've no idea what she meant by that, but I'll have plenty of time with her to find out."

"Those men, they wanted you because of what you are, not who you are. What I mean is, they needed you for your surgical abilities." Ivy nodded, looking over at Aunt Bea. "Did you hear what Henry called the other man? He's someone that they've been looking for a few decades. He's been the cause of a lot of deaths."

"He told me that the world would never know about this either. That the men here today with him have been briefed and briefed again to make sure that they know it." Ivy looked at him and he felt her pain. "They hurt her, those men. They did more than just put a few explosives under her skin—they ruined her financially, too. She has nothing left. Just as I had done to me."

He'd forgotten that, that she'd lost everything in a fire. Evan looked over at his aunt and wondered why she'd not reached out to any of them before today. When Ivy laughed a little, he asked her what was so funny.

"She told me out there, before you got her brought here by Tanner, that she fought with me that day to see if I would stand up to her. Then she told me that once she felt not anger from me, but a seriousness and conviction that astounded Bea, she knew that on some level I'd be all right. But she thought for sure she was dead. And no one would know that she'd never meant to be the mean old aunt that everyone hated to have around."

"I'll make sure that she knows that we'll be here for her forever." Ivy nodded, and he stood up. "I can smell all that food in the other room. She'll be all right until she wakes, which won't be long, and we can join the family."

Just as they were leaving the room, he turned in time to see Ivy kiss his aunt on the forehead. When they left the room together, he took one more look back and saw his aunt smile. Evan knew that his family had gotten another member today. He only hoped that they could all survive her as they had the criminals that had messed with his aunt.

Before You Go...

HELP AN AUTHOR

write a review

THANK YOU!

Share your voice and help guide other readers to these wonderful books. Even if it's only a line or two your reviews help readers discover the author's books so they can continue creating stories that you'll love. Login to your favorite retailer and leave a review. Thank you.

AWARD WINNING, BESTSELLING AUTHOR

Kathi Barton, winner of the Pinnacle Book Achievement award as well as a best-selling author on Amazon and All Romance books, lives in Nashport, Ohio with her husband Paul. When not creating new worlds and romance, Kathi and her husband enjoy camping and going to auctions. She can also be seen at county fairs with her husband who is an artist and potter.

Her muse, a cross between Jimmy Stewart and Hugh Jackman, brings her stories to life for her readers in a way that has them coming back time and again for more. Her favorite genre is paranormal romance with a great deal of spice. You can visit Kathi online and drop her an email if you'd like. She loves hearing from her fans. aaronskiss@gmail.com.

Follow Kathi on her blog: http://kathisbartonauthor.blogspot.com/